ENEMY AT THE DOOR

STEPHEN TAYLOR

www.dissectdesigns.com

ISBN: 978-1-917616-17-1

DANNY PEARSON
WILL RETURN

For updates about current and upcoming releases, as well as exclusive promotions, visit the authors website at:

www.stephentaylorbooks.com

ALSO BY STEPHEN TAYLOR
THE DANNY PEARSON THRILLER SERIES

Vodka Over London Ice

Execution of Faith

Who Holds The Power

Alive Until I Die

Sport of Kings

Blood Runs Deep

Command to Kill

No Upper Limit

Leave Nothing To Chance

Won't Stay dead

Till Death Do Us Part

Enemy At The Door

Whatever it takes

CHAPTER 1

anny walked past the Crimea and Indian Mutiny Memorial statue sitting in a small square in front of the imposing façade of Westminster Abbey. He weaved impatiently through the usual crowds of tourists that bottlenecked around the Abbey, all the way to the houses of Parliament with Westminster Bridge spanning the Thames behind it. Danny glanced at his watch and frowned. He was late, and he hated being late.

Emerging from the crowd of tourists all looking up at Big Ben through the cameras on their phones, Danny crossed the road and walked quickly along Parliament Street to his destination, the Red Lion pub. The pub, with its black façade and traditional gold brewery signage, had sat on that street corner for almost five hundred years and was heaving with lunchtime drinkers sitting on the benches outside, with even more people visible on the inside through the pub's windows. Danny entered, walking along the hard-as-concrete oak floorboards seasoned over the years with a million splashes of spilt beer trodden in by a million feet. He headed up the stairs to a dining room clad in warm oak panelling that surrounded the solid oak flooring and tables, where customers sat below a highly decorative patterned ceiling lit up with brass chandeliers. Scanning the room, Danny spotted Scott sitting at a table with three men. He recognised two of them from somewhere, probably from the news. Being so close to the Houses of Parliament, its members often frequented the pub. He couldn't remember their names or what they were the ministers of. Seeing him, Scott grinned, got up and shook their hands before saying his goodbyes and heading over.

'I say, old man, you're unusually late. I'd almost given up on you,' said Scott over the hum of conversation in the busy pub.

'Yeah, sorry, mate, engineering work on the Tube again, lots of delays. Have you finished your meeting?'

'Yes, yes, it was only an informal chat with the Minister for Technology and a couple of other hush-hush type chaps, the good and bad world of artificial intelligence and cybercrime, all that sort of thing. Now, I'd say eat here, but it's rather busy and there's a wait for food orders.'

'Ok, let's go somewhere quieter,' said Danny, turning to head downstairs and out of the pub.

Once they were out on the pavement, they headed away from the drinkers outside until they could hear each other over the chatter.

'I know a pub a little way past Westminster Abbey. It should be quieter than here,' said Scott, taking the lead.

They'd only taken a few paces down Parliament Street when a deafening boom erupted from behind them. The pavement below their feet shook a millisecond before a shockwave of hot air, glass and debris slammed into their backs, forcing them to stumble forward.

Danny planted his feet on the pavement, finding his balance fast. Standing tall, he turned amongst a panicked crowd of cowering and screaming people. He took in the pub's glassless windows and gutted interior. Smoke poured from within, thinning occasionally to show small pockets of fire tearing at seat covers and curtains.

Turning in a slow circle, Danny looked at the injured and frightened people trying to get away from the scene. Working from left to right, he scanned the crowd on the opposite side of the road. His eyes flicked from face to face, spending less than a second on each one to register the shock, horror, fear and other natural emotions you'd expect from witnessing such an atrocity. He flicked onto one face, then off, stopping to look back when his subconscious told him something was out of place. A bearded man stood perfectly still amongst the crowd, staring intently at the pub, studying it with no emotion. He looked to be thirty to thirty-five, his short ginger beard making it difficult to determine an exact age. He was of similar height and build to Danny, but stood with his shoulders purposely rolled forward, stooping slightly to make himself look smaller and more invisible in a crowd. A tuft of curly ginger hair was just visible from under the pulled-up hood of his blue, lightweight Nike jacket.

As if feeling Danny's gaze, the man's eyes flicked off the destroyed pub, locking with Danny's as he stood tall and calm above the panicking crowd. The link between the two of them only lasted for a fraction of a second. At that moment, Danny knew without a shadow of a doubt that the man was military or ex-military. The sharp eyes and emotionless expression as he calculated his next move gave it away. Showing no outward sign that he'd noticed Danny, he turned sharply and nimbly weaved his way smoothly through the crowd of onlookers transfixed by the devastated pub. His retreat through the crowd was only visible by glimpses of the blue hood and red rucksack on his back, swinging from side to side as he picked up speed.

Oh no you don't.

'Stay there, I'll be back,' Danny shouted to Scott, already

halfway across the road in pursuit of the man he suspected had something to do with the explosion.

'Back, what? What the hell's going on?' Scott shouted after him, his head swinging from the injured outside the pub to Danny as he disappeared into the crowd on the opposite side of the road.

Keeping his eyes glued on the flashes of red rucksack as it dipped in and out of view amongst the crowd, Danny started gaining on his target. With the sound of approaching sirens filling the air, the blue hood did a ninety-degree turn, followed by the red rucksack, as his target changed direction.

The guy came into full view as he darted out of the crowd and ran across Parliament Street, heading toward Westminster Bridge. Danny pushed out of the crowd, his foot hitting the road for a split second before having to jump back onto the pavement as a stream of police and paramedic first responder vehicles flew past, missing him by inches. Almost touching the back of the last vehicle, Danny sprinted across the road, ignoring the beeping traffic as he stayed on the edge of the road rather than the pavement, avoiding the crowds to close the increased gap between him and his target.

Another flash of rucksack changing direction caused Danny to curse. His target flew down the steps opposite Big Ben into the depths of Westminster Tube station. Following, Danny leaped down the steps and stumbled into the ticket hall, causing commuters and tourists to flinch and jump out of the way. Spinning around in the middle of the open space at all the different entrances to train platforms, Danny caught sight of the rucksack man tapping his ticket before passing through the station barriers and heading down the escalators. Not wanting to lose sight of him, Danny dodged around the line of commuters filing through the ticket barriers and hurdled over the top of the metal bar. Ignoring the shouts from the station staff behind him, Danny pushed past people as he hurried down the moving escalators. Alerted by the shouts from above, the blue hooded man turned so he could see behind him, a brief look of surprise flashing across his face at the sight of Danny careering down the escalator towards him.

Charging down the last few steps, Danny jumped off the escalators and darted through the tiled archway leading to the Circle line eastbound platform. Barely five seconds later, Danny entered the platform, sliding to an abrupt stop when he found it packed full of people trying to squeeze onto a newly arrived tube train. He hung back, looking up and down the platform, trying to spot his man. The beeps sounded for the doors about to close, forcing him to decide, stay or get on. Danny jumped into the train as they slid shut.

Once inside, he moved his head from side to side, trying to see around the standing passengers towards the back of the train. There was no sign of him, the blue hood or the rucksack. While turning to look towards the front of the train, Danny came face to face with his target standing less than three feet away from him on the platform outside the closed door. He had his phone up in front of him and was clicking off picture after picture of Danny through the glass. As the train pulled away, he lowered the phone and locked eyes with Danny, their colour an unnaturally bright blue. His mouth curled into a smile and he winked before turning away. A second later the train left the platform, with just the blackness of the underground tunnel whizzing past the window. Danny was still staring at the same point on the glass when the lights of the Embankment Tube station and its platform opened up before his eyes a few minutes later. Stepping out as the doors opened, Danny walked amongst the crowd toward the exit, looking for the sign for the westbound platform to catch the next train back to Westminster station and where he left Scott standing outside the pub.

'Armed police, put your hands where I can see them and get down on the ground now!'

Danny looked puzzled at London's counter-terrorism officers, pointing their G36 assault rifles in his direction. He turned his head to see who they were talking to. When the other passengers moved away from him like he had the plague, he realised they were talking to him.

'Put your hands where we can see them and get down on the ground. Now!' A clearly agitated officer in charge shouted for a second time.

Danny raised his hands slowly and slid down onto his knees, then onto his chest. The second he was down, officers pounced on him, their knees wedged into the middle of his back while they pulled his hands behind him and secured them in handcuffs.

'Fuck me, fellas, this is a bit strong for fare dodging, isn't it?' Danny said, as they grabbed him on either side and hoisted him off the floor onto his feet.

The joke didn't go down well. After being told they were arresting him on suspicion of terrorism, they marched him out of the Tube station and hustled him into the back of a police car which immediately accelerated away, sirens wailing.

CHAPTER 2

After being processed in the custody suite at New Scotland Yard, officers took Danny into a window-less room and made him strip. An officer gave him a full body search while another officer bagged his clothes in an evidence bag. Danny kept his annoyance hidden. He said nothing and showed no emotion. When they'd finished, he pulled on the paper boiler suit they provided. He'd made a mental note of the time on the clock above the custody desk when they arrived and was keeping track of how long they'd been there from glancing at the officers' watches as they hustled him through the station.

They took him into a gloomy interview room and left him handcuffed to a ring fixed in the centre of a bolted-down table. Still counting the minutes off in his head, Danny stared defiantly at the large, mirrored observation window to one side of him. After approximately ten minutes, the door opened and two suited men entered. They circled slowly around the table, placing a laptop on the opposite side to him before dragging their chairs noisily across the concrete floor for effect. They sat down in unison, giving Danny the standard, intimidating interview stare before speaking.

'Detective Chief Inspector Ian Monroe and Detective Inspector Robert Aimes in attendance. We are interviewing Daniel Pearson regarding the bombing of the Red Lion public house on Parliament Street, Westminster,' DCI Ian Monroe said for the benefit of the recording equipment.

Danny sat opposite, looked across the table at DCI Monroe, unimpressed, and yawned as he continued to caution him with the "anything you may say may be taken in evidence," speech.

'Mr Pearson, you entered the Red Lion public house at 12:36pm, then left with a Mr Scott Miller at 12:58pm. At exactly 1:00pm an explosive device detonated, following which you fled the scene, heading into Westminster Tube station where you tried to leave the area on an eastbound Circle line Tube train,' stated DI Robert Aimes.

'I know where I went, because I fucking went there, didn't I?' Danny growled, looking at DI Aimes angrily before taking a breath and continuing. 'If you bothered to look at your CCTV footage of the area, you'd see I was chasing a suspect. Ginger beard, blue Nike top with the hood up, red rucksack. Any of this ringing any bells?'

The two men looked at the laptop while DI Aimes tapped at the keys, presumably searching through camera footage. After a minute or so, they looked up, their faces giving nothing away.

'So, Mr Pearson, you arrived at the pub at 12:36 carrying a black Adidas sports holdall. When you left the public house at 12:58, you didn't have it. What was in the holdall, Mr Pearson, and why didn't you leave with it?' DCI Monroe said, leaning in to give Danny a 'we've got you bang to rights' stare as he tried to unnerve him.

More annoyed than unnerved, Danny frowned at the DCI.
'Show me,' he said in a calm voice.
The DCI spun the laptop around to face Danny and leaned

over to hit the enter key. A crystal clear CCTV shot from opposite the pub showed Danny walking quickly down Parliament Street before entering it. Only in this footage he was carrying a black sports holdall with the white Adidas trademark stripes.

'Show me the other footage, the one where I'm leaving,' Danny demanded.

The two detectives looked at each other, slightly taken aback by Danny driving the direction of the interview. When he couldn't think of a good reason not to show it, the DCI reached over and tapped a few keys to bring up and play footage from multiple cameras.

Danny and Scott left the pub. The bomb went off and Danny ran through the crowd, heading towards Westminster Bridge before heading down into the Tube station. Only in this footage, the man with the red rucksack was nowhere to be seen.

The muscles in Danny's cheeks flexed as he ground his teeth and stared intensely at the footage. When it was over, he sat back in the chair as far as he could with his hands cuffed to the table and said nothing. The DCI spun the laptop back around, the look on his face giving away the notion that he thought they had their man, case closed.

'Right, shall we start again? An explosive device was in the sports holdall, wasn't it? Are you working alone, or are you part of a bigger organisation?' DCI Monroe said. His manner was more telling Danny than asking him.

'What time is it?' Danny said calmly.

'Why, have you got somewhere you need to be? Someone you need to see? Trust me, Mr Pearson, until I get some answers you're not going anywhere,' said DI Aimes, doing his best to look intimidating.

'Is Scott Miller here?' Danny said, ignoring Aimes as he turned his attention to Monroe.

'Yes, Mr Miller is in the interview room next door. He hasn't stopped asking for Earl Grey tea and biscuits. Now, can we get back to the bag and why you blew up the Red Lion public house, killing over twenty people?' DCI Monroe said, his voice raised.

'Any second now, a man is going to come through that door and order you to release me,' Danny said, glimpsing Monroe's watch as he instinctively glanced at it when the subject of time was mentioned.

The detectives looked at each other, bemused smiles crossing their faces.

'No one's going to get you out of this one, Mr Pearson. Just do yourself a favour and tell us why you did it. I'll ask you again, are you working alone? Is Mr Miller part of this? Or are you part of some little disgruntled group trying to get back at the establishment?'

As DCI Monroe opened his mouth to continue, the door opened abruptly, stopping him in his tracks.

The government man known only as Simon entered the room, immaculately dressed in a handmade navy blue Savile Row suit. Power and authority emanated from him.

'Ah, there you are, Daniel. DCI Monroe, I believe. If you wouldn't mind removing Mr Pearson's handcuffs, there's a good fellow.'

'What? Wait. Who the hell are you?' DCI Monroe spluttered.

Simon just stood to one side with a polite smile on his face. New Scotland Yard's chief superintendent entering the room from behind him.

'Ian, just do as he says,' he snapped.

'Thank you, Derrick. If you could get somebody to release Mr Miller and return their clothes and personal effects, that would be most helpful.'

Ignoring the chief superintendent's look of annoyance at being ordered about, Simon turned and left the room.

'I'll be outside when you are ready, Daniel. Don't be all day about it. We have lots to do,' Simon said as he walked away.

'You heard the man,' Danny said, rattling the handcuffs at DCI Monroe.

Out of the paper boiler suit and back into his own clothes, Danny caught up with Scott as they left the station.

'I say, Daniel, what on earth is going on? I feel violated. They strip searched me. Me! Like a common criminal. Then they kept asking me questions about you, and a black bag, and who you know. To cap it all, my new Armani suit is all creased,' Scott said, trying to smooth the creases out of his jacket from where it had been bagged as evidence.

'If you wanted to alter a CCTV image in real time, say, to give someone a black bag they didn't have or to make a person disappear, how would you do it?' Danny said, spotting Simon's driver opening the rear door of his car for them to get in.

'Mmm, that would require a lot of computing power and resources. I mean, first you'd have to hack the original feed, map the image you wanted to alter, then let AI digitally change it on the fly. There would be a delay, of course, the length of which would depend on your resources. Let me think. If I linked my systems together, I could probably alter a feed with only a two hundredths of a second delay.'

'What about multiple feeds at the same time? Six, maybe eight or ten feeds, one after another,' Danny said, getting into the back of Simon's car.

'Oh, hello Simon. Er, up to ten CCTV feeds. If, and I mean if, you could hack the servers that host the CCTV feeds and take it over undetected. You would need a huge computer mainframe and some very sophisticated artificial intelligence software. Something like the computer systems at the SIS building. I imagine that could probably handle it,' Scott said as Danny and Simon listened.

'Good afternoon, Mr Miller. On that insightful note, shall we be off? The SIS building please, Arthur,' Simon said to his driver.

CHAPTER 3

After checking both ways, the man Danny had chased into Westminster Tube station ducked down a narrow one-way access street. He looked up at the rear of the modern six-storey apartment block towering above him on one side. Heading along the street until he was satisfied that nobody was paying him any attention. When he was around halfway down, he ducked in between a collection of large commercial rubbish bins and crouched down. Sliding the red rucksack off his back, he placed it at his feet, then took the lightweight Nike sports jacket off and placed it on the floor beside him. A SIG Sauer M18 handgun swung in its shoulder holster as he bent forward to open the rucksack. He pulled a sealed plastic bag out and ripped it open. Removing a lightweight beige jacket from inside, he shook the creases out before putting it on, zipping it up to hide the gun.

Reaching back into the rucksack, he removed a small box with a digital display on the front, his knuckles brushing a rough, powdery substance coating the inside of the rucksack as he pulled his hand out. Leaning forward to see around the bins, he checked the street was still empty, then tucked himself back under cover. Putting his hand on his head, he gripped his curly ginger hair and pulled it until the wig slid free, revealing a neatly cut head of light brown hair. He put the wig in the rucksack, then peeled the fake beard from his face to place it in the bag with the wig. Putting his fingers to his eyes, he gently pinched out the blue contact lenses to reveal his natural brown eyes. After dropping them in the bag, he unzipped the pocket on the front of the rucksack and pulled out a small GPS tracker. He stamped on it with the heel of his shoe, making sure it was dead before dropping it in with the other items. He set the timer on the small device for 60 seconds and placed it on top of the other items in the rucksack. Closing it, he stood up and walked out from between the bins, casually heading back towards the main road. Reaching into the inside pocket of the beige jacket, he pulled out a new baseball hat and a pair of sunglasses and put them on. Pulling the peak down low, he rounded the corner and walked amongst the flow of people, invisible in plain sight.

Back between the bins, the timer hit zero and the accelerant in the small device ignited, instantly setting off a chain reaction between the potassium chlorate and phosphorus sulphide coated material on the inside of the rucksack. A super bright flame flared through the top of the rucksack, reaching several feet high until the 1200°C phosphorus sulphide burnt off, leaving the polypropylene rucksack and its contents reduced into a smouldering lump of melted sludge.

A quarter of a mile away the man crossed Chicheley Street, looking down at the London eye dominating the skyline at its far end. Despite his destination being on the opposite side of the road, he kept on walking. He scanned every pedestrian and vehicle that passed for something out of place, moving his eyes and not his head as he checked reflections in glass doors and windows for anyone following behind him.

Satisfied that he was alone, he crossed the road and turned back on himself walking until he reached the apartment building where he was staying. He entered the foyer and took the stairs rather than the lift to the top floor. Pausing at the fire door at the top of the stairs, he looked through the small glass window to check the corridor was clear before entering. Reaching the apartment door, he tapped the number provided by the Airbnb booking onto the stainless steel buttons on the door lock, twisted the handle and went inside.

The modern two-bedroom apartment was minimalistic, bright and clean. He paced over to the far side of the apartment and looked out over the terrace through the wall-to-wall glass folding doors giving priceless views of the London Eye and London's iconic skyline towering above the neighbouring buildings. Tearing himself away, he moved to a small occasional table in the room's corner and removed a tiny camera stuck to the base of a lamp. He turned it off to stop its motion sensor, triggered by his arrival into the apartment, from continuing to make the phone in his pocket buzz, as it sent him an intruder alert and live video stream to the device. Placing the camera down onto the dining table, he took a seat and inserted a mobile USB internet dongle into a robust field laptop. He opened the laptop lid and turned it on, typing in a password to connect the internet dongle via a secure VPN.

Three and a half thousand miles away, a computer in an apartment he rented in New York burst into life and bridged his connection via another secure VPN to a dusty computer sitting in a small office he rented in Atlantic City, the chain making tracing him an almost impossible task. With the connections complete, his dark web encrypted contact screen appeared. He logged in with the name Colorado and typed.

Contract completed. I trust my anonymity is intact.

. . .

He waited a minute or two, watching the screen until the cursor started blinking and a new message scrolled its way across the screen.

The masking test was a success. Your image was completely removed from all government and traffic cameras in the area. Thank you for the facial pictures. Your pursuer will be busy with the authorities for a very long time.

He smiled as he read the message, then started typing.

Our business has concluded. Payment is now due.

This time, the message came straight back.

Transferring payment now.

Followed a few moments later by:

Transfer complete.

As he put his hand on top of the laptop, ready to close it down, a new message scrolled across the screen, stopping him.

I have another job I would like to discuss with you, if you are interested?

He paused for a moment to think about it, eventually reaching for the keyboard to answer.

Details?

After a few seconds, the message

Details to follow shortly.

came back.

I will send you a new link, contact name is now Montana. The link will be open for 24 hours only.

As soon as he sent the message, he logged out, the disconnection automatically putting the remote computers into sleep mode, severing any means of tracking him.

CHAPTER 4

Danny frowned at the missed call notifications from his wife, Nikki, as he placed his phone, keys, and change in a grey plastic tray. A security guard slid the tray away onto a conveyor belt which ran through an airport style x-ray machine. Another security guard waved Danny toward him from the other side of a large metal detector to clear security and enter the Secret Intelligence building and home of Military Intelligence, Section 6, or MI6 as it is more commonly known. After collecting his personal effects, Danny reluctantly followed Simon into the lift. When they exited onto the sixth floor, he hung back to return Nikki's calls.

'Danny, thank god. I saw the explosion on the news and when I couldn't get hold of you and Scott, I thought the worst. Oh, no, Scott! Is he with you? Is he ok? Where have you been? I've been worried sick,' Nikki blurted out, hours of pent up anxiety spilling out of her.

With all the chaos, Danny had forgotten that he told her he was meeting Scott in the Red Lion pub near the Houses of Parliament.

'It's alright, love, we're both fine. We were lucky. We left the pub just before it went up. Sorry, this is the first chance I've had to call you. Me and Scott got arrested in all the chaos. We've only just been released,' Danny said, in his best calm-and-reassuring, it-was-nothing voice, while following Simon into the MI6 operations room.

'What, the police? That's ridiculous. Do you need me to come and get you?' Nikki said, her voice calming down now she knew they were ok.

'No, Simon got us out. I'm over at MI6 now.'

'MI6, why? Are you in trouble?' she said, the anxiety rising again.

'No, no, I'm just helping them out. There's a possibility that I ran into the bomber outside the pub. Look, we're both ok so you can relax. I don't know how long I'll be here. It could be late, so don't wait up. I'll get a cab home when I'm done here,' Danny said, conscious that Simon, Scott and head of the Secret Intelligence Service, Edward Jenkins were all staring, waiting for him to finish.

'Ok, I'm just relieved you're safe. Oh, and Danny?'

'What?'

'I love you.'

Danny turned away from Scott, Simon, and Edward. 'Yeah, I love you too,' he said quietly before hanging up and turning back to them.

'Right, now that we have everyone's attention, Edward, would you mind showing us what you have, please?' said Simon, turning away from Danny to look at the wall of giant screens covering the far side of the operations room.

'Of course,' replied Edward, giving the nod to one of his operatives sitting close by at their computer terminal.

Four of the giant screens transformed into a grid of twelve CCTV feeds, the footage replaying Danny's journey past Westminster Abbey and the Houses of Parliament on his way to the Red Lion public house from a multitude of cameras and angles. In each one, he was carrying the black sports holdall with the white Adidas trademark stripes.

'I say, that's most impressive. Great digital rendering. It must be a sixth, possibly seventh generation AI model. I say Edward, old man, could we expand the screen on the bottom right?' said Scott enthusiastically.

Edward turned and nodded to his man. A few seconds later, the image of Danny appeared as one massive picture across all four screens.

'Mmm, that is really rather good. Are you sure you didn't have a sports bag with you, Daniel?' Scott said, grinning at Danny.

'That's not funny, Scott,' Danny muttered grumpily, giving Scott a stern look.

'Stop, go back a few seconds,' Scott said, ignoring Danny's comment. 'Stop there, that's it. Now zoom in on the boot of that black cab, that's it. Closer, closer, stop. Can we enhance that a touch?' Scott said to the operative at his desk as if he was in control of the operations room.

The operative looked across at Edward, who nodded for him to go ahead. He tapped a few keys and MI6's multi-million pound, state-of-the-art computer system enhanced the section of footage around the boot of the cab to give a clear, if not slightly stretched reflection of Danny on the curved boot as he passed on the pavement beside it. There was no bag in the reflection.

'As you can see, the AI generator has recognised and calculated the appropriate reflection on less challenging reflective surfaces, windows, glass doors, polished metal, rendering the bag in the reflection as it should be. But because of the image distortion and muted colours in the reflection on the taxicab's boot, it has failed to recognise it and adjust the feed, hence no bag. Intelligent but not that intelligent,' Scott finished with a certain amount of smugness.

'Mmm, yes, so it would seem. Shall we move on to the

footage from directly after the explosion?' Simon said, his mind ticking over why it took Scott less than five minutes to find a flaw in the altered footage, when a room full of agents and analysts had been trawling over the footage for the past four hours.

'Can we have the footage from after the explosion, please?' Edward called across to his operative.

All the screens went blank before bursting back into life with over twenty feeds, the right-hand section covering Danny from multiple angles as he ran from the Red Lion pub along Parliament Street, crossing the road to head off towards Westminster Bridge. The grid of feeds on the left-hand side of the screens displayed his journey through Westminster Tube station as he crossed the ticket hall, headed down the escalators into a central tunnel before moving out onto the platform and boarding the Tube train.

'Daniel, old man, how far ahead of you was this fellow you were chasing?' Scott said, without taking his eyes from the feeds.

'Er, it varied, somewhere between ten and twenty metres. But when the Tube train pulled away, he was right outside the window taking pictures of me,' Danny said, amazed that he couldn't see any sign of the man in the multitude of camera feeds.

'Pictures, you say. Mmm, they used them to digitally map your face and find the footage of you travelling to the pub. Detailed pictures make it quicker and easier to alter the recorded image to give you the bag,' Scott said.

'But how can you make someone disappear across twenty plus feeds from multiple sources in real time?' Simon asked.

'Let me see. First, you image map your subject, in this case our ginger haired bomber friend. Then you need your AI system to track the subject's location, probably via a GPS tracker. The AI then cross references the subject's location with the location of the cameras. It locks on to the subject with image recognition, then wipes him from existence. Our AI altered feed is recorded onto the system's hard drive instead of the real one, their system dropping its access to each camera as our subject moves out of coverage, accessing the next camera as he comes into that one's field of vision. Fairly simple, actually. The really impressive bit is how they gained access to the multiple server providers that manage and host the cameras for traffic, security and the underground. But your question shouldn't be how they did it, your question should be who has the technical ability and systems capability to do this, and the obvious, why bother?' Scott said.

'Why bother?' Simon said, turning to look at Scott.

'Yes, why bother? The bomber, terrorist, whatever you want to call him, he could, or maybe he did, wear a disguise. There was nobody looking for him when he arrived at the pub, and nobody knew who he was or where he was going when he left the scene of the crime. I think this was a test run, a show of power. Whoever did this was more intent on showing you that they could do it, rather than they had to do it.'

Simon said nothing for a while. He turned from Scott and stared at the wall of screens, deep in thought, before turning to Danny.

'Daniel, the man you chased, did he look like he was wearing a disguise?'

Before answering, Danny shut his eyes and took a minute to recall a detailed image of the man standing outside of the Tube train.

'He was a professional, almost certainly ex-military, probably Special Forces. If a professional's real hair was ginger, they'd have dyed it to some sort of unremarkable mid-brown colour to blend in with the majority of the local population. Yeah, it was almost certainly a wig and a false beard. He could have been wearing coloured contact lenses as well.'

CHAPTER 5

Reaching the doors of the modern technology building, Silus Montague turned around to look back across the grounds of the sixteenth century St Peter's College, Cambridge. It was early evening and free from any students as all classes were over for the day and the building was a fair distance from the student accommodation block. Satisfied he wasn't overlooked, Silus unlocked the door to the technology building and went inside, locking the door behind him.

As dean of the college, Silus knew the building would be free of after college clubs and teachers working late, because he'd booked the building out for server and system maintenance. He hurried along the dim corridors lit by emergency lighting, opting to leave the main lights off in case they drew attention from the outside. As he approached the information and communication technology department, a light from within room 1.23 beamed out through the small square pane of glass in the door, highlighting a row of lockers on the opposite side of the corridor. He paused before going in, gathering his thoughts. The pub bombing hadn't gone the way he'd expected it to, and now he was going to have to put a spin on it if he was going to justify the actions of the man pulling the strings and keep the students in that room on track - and keep them on track he must if he was to get his payday and the new life he deserved.

As he entered, three faces appeared from behind their computer monitors on the far side of the room. A young woman with green hair, heavy black eyeliner, and a ring that disappeared into each nostril to join through a pierced septum above her black lipsticked lips shared a look of self-confident annoyance with a shoulder-length, curly brown-haired student showing his clenched teeth through a patchy attempt at a beard. The third student looked like the odd one out, with neatly cut short hair and an anxious look on his clean-shaven face, his eyes darting between the other students and the professor through his little round glasses.

'What the fuck, Professor? The pub was supposed to be empty when the bomb went off. People died,' the shoulder-length, curly brown-haired student said, his voice raised as he threw his hands up in the air angrily.

'Yeah, people will think we're murderers,' the green-haired woman joined in while the third student stood staring nervously in Silus's direction.

Silus held his palms up to pacify them.

'It's regrettable, I agree. Our benefactor anonymously called the authorities and reported the bomb. But they didn't take it seriously, and this is the result, Sebastian,' Silus lied, continuing after a pause when he saw their faces soften a little. 'This is why our cause is so important. Nothing works in this country. We gave them a chance, and they blew it. Nobody's going to think you're a murderer, Rachael. Did you set the bomb off? No, you didn't. That mistake is on our bene-factor and ally. When our campaign succeeds and he comes out of the shadows to head Genesis UK, he will take responsi-bility for his actions and justify why they had to be done. It was a necessary action to open the eyes of our nation.'

Silus smiled warmly as the students relaxed and sat back down behind their computers. The fatherly relationship and the trust he'd groomed into the hand-picked students making them hang on his every word and believe everything he said.

'Are you alright, Tobias?' Silus asked, the anxious look on Tobias's face still looking back at him.

'He's fine, aren't you, Tobias?' Sebastian said, throwing Tobias a look that made him nod and return to his keyboard without having the nerve to speak his mind.

'Good, what happened at the pub wasn't perfect, but we can't let it spoil our moment. This is your day, the day to come out of the shadows and let everyone know who you are and what you stand for. So, are you ready?'

'Yes, Professor. I've hacked the individual security protocols and created back doors through remote servers. Rachael's got all the virtual private networks in place with masked internet protocols and Tobias has the media file ready for simultaneous broadcast,' Sebastian boasted, the natural leader over the other two.

'Then there's nothing left to do other than show them who's really in control,' Silus beamed, the students lapping up his approval.

CHAPTER 6

'Sir, sir, someone's hacked the TV broadcast,' came a shout from across the MI6 operations room.

'Which network?' Edward demanded.

'All of them, sir.'

'Put it up on screen,'

The multiple feeds disappeared off the large main screen to be replaced by a slim, good looking, middle-aged man in an expensive suit sitting in an oak panelled room of a stately home.

'Citizens of Britain, no matter who has been in power, your government has been failing you for decades. Over one in five people in the UK are in poverty, the National Minimum Wage and zero-hour contracts have become the reality for the majority. Honest, hard-working people are unable to feed, clothe or put a roof over their families' heads. Water companies poison our rivers, electric and gas companies hold us to ransom with over-inflated prices. Storms, floods and drought ravage our country because the government chooses money and profit and self preservation over tackling global warming and environmental destruction. We are close to the point of no return. Our planet is in decline and this will lead to the extinction of the human race.'

'Who is that man? He looks familiar. Are you running him through the database?' Simon barked across the room at no one in particular.

'There's no point,' Danny said, turning away from the screen to look at Simon.

'What? Why?'

'Because that's Daniel Craig, you know the actor, 007, James Bond, Casino Royale,' Danny replied bluntly.

'They call it deepfake. You scan a face into the computer and it maps it with thousands of data points, then you just take the face, in this case Daniel Craig's, put it over your own, the artificial intelligence program links it to your own data points so it moves as you move. Add a quick sample of Mr. Craig's voice into the system and, well, you can see the result,' said Scott, gesturing toward the broadcast in front of them.

'Today we stepped out of the shadows and struck a blow for you, the people of Britain. Democracy isn't working, not because of you and me, because we only have the choices they want us to have. The parties, the government, the establishment are corrupt, money and power drive their decisions. They don't care about what's best for you and me and the planet we rely on. The Genesis UK movement has begun. The time for action is now. Genesis UK wants to ensure we all have a future. Genesis UK wants your support.'

When Daniel Craig stopped talking, he lifted his arm and clicked his fingers. In the same breath, the power went out, leaving everyone standing in silence amongst the dead screens and computers, the room faintly lit by a grey green light from the battery powered emergency lighting system. A second later, the building's generators kicked in and lights and machinery blinked and whirred back into life. Simon looked around the windowless room before hurrying out into the corridor, followed by Edward, Danny, and Scott. They stood by the stairs looking through the windows, out across the Thames at the dark London skyline.

'They've taken out the entire National Grid,' said Simon.

As they watched, the streetlights and buildings burst back into the illuminated normality we all take for granted. It was at that point mobile phones started pinging and beeping with received messages, not just some phones, but all the mobile phones.

Danny slid his out of his pocket and read the message.

Genesis UK will give you the future you deserve. Genesis UK is the future. Join us and change the world.

'Quite the introduction,' Simon muttered after reading the message. A crease appearing on his forehead as he thought about the events of the day before looking up from his phone at Danny and Scott.

'Scott, I'd like you to cancel any plans for the immediate future. Your technical knowledge is invaluable and we need to shut Genesis UK down fast.'

'Certainly, old man, as long as you agree to pay my usual fee for services rendered,' said Scott, looking Simon straight in the eye.

'Agreed. Daniel, you are the only one to have seen the bomber in the flesh. I'd like you to come in tomorrow and run through the footage and any matching candidates on our database,' Simon said, turning to Danny.

Danny's dislike for the government man would normally have made him refuse, but there was something about the man he'd chased that made him want to find him. The fact that he'd got away from him so easily played on his mind, and the smile and wink from outside the Tube train window, goading him as it pulled away, annoyed the hell out of him.

Without saying a word, Danny nodded his agreement before they all headed back into the operations room.

CHAPTER 7

itting in his home office, Alfred Birchwood watched streaming TV feeds while monitoring a host of open windows, their streams of scrolling data spread across three large monitors spanning the desk in front of him. He flicked his wrist to watch the second hand tick on his Rolex submariner watch, smiling to himself when the TV feeds abruptly cut off to be replaced by the deepfake image of Daniel Craig at precisely seven o'clock.

Uninterested in the message being delivered by the famous actor, Birchwood left the volume down on the streams and turned his attention to the windows full of streaming data. His servers in the Birchwood Technologies building located on Cambridge's renowned science park were handling the massive amount of bandwidth Genesis UK's takeover broadcast required with ease. He turned his attention to another window. A smaller system he'd generously donated to the prestigious St Peter's College, Cambridge, was running high at 78%. His eyes flicked across to catch the end of the TV broadcast, with Daniel Craig clicking his fingers. A split second later, the power went off. Birchwood didn't move. He sat in the dark room staring at the screens illuminating his face. His UPS battery backup system continued to power his computer systems and ultra high-speed internet connection.

After watching the demands on Birchwood Technologies' and St Peter's College servers drop at the end of the TV feed hack, he watched them spike as Genesis UK overloaded the National Grid systems, fooling them into thinking there was a massive power surge which caused a temporary system shutdown. Like clockwork, demand dropped as the power came back on around him, before spiking for the last time as Genesis took over the UK cellular transmitters and sent a message to all, making the mobile phone on his desk buzz with the incoming Genesis UK message.

When it was over, Birchwood spent a few minutes checking his security measures. Satisfied the evening's activities were untraceable, he breathed out deeply and stretched back in his chair. After a minute or two, he reached forward and picked up his phone. Ignoring the message from Genesis UK, he selected Professor Silus Montague's contact and hit the call button. A window opened up in the top corner of his computer screen, showing that the call was being diverted through a voice over an internet encryption program.

'Alfred,' said Montague after only one ring.

'Congratulations, Professor, the first phase of our plan went perfectly. How are our young geniuses holding up?' Birchwood said, his tone jovial.

'Naturally, they are not happy about the deaths at the Red Lion public house, which has made them even more impatient to know the identity of their anonymous benefactor.'

'And what did you tell them?' Birchwood said, taking a more serious tone.

'My reply was exactly as we planned. You are a high-ranking member of parliament who supports the radical need for change to protect all our futures. You cannot reveal your-self until Genesis UK has gained enough support to over-throw the government, and the bombing was necessary to add a physical weight to the cyber attacks, which will make the government sit up and take notice.'

'And they bought that?'

'Yes, I have their trust. Although Tobias is struggling a little with the pub bombing and its subsequent loss of life.'

'Mmm, is he going to be a problem?' Birchwood said, concern edging into his voice.

'No, no, Rachael and Sebastian are keeping him in line. Tobias looks to Sebastian as an older brother. He'll do anything he says,' said Montague quickly.

'He'd better, Silus. I've got too much riding on this to let some silver spoon-fed little prick ruin everything.'

'I assure you it's all under control, Alfred.'

'Make sure it is. You wouldn't want your retirement in the sun to be replaced by one behind bars, would you?' Birch-wood said, listening to the silence as the gravity of his words hit the professor.

'It won't be a problem,' came a sombre reply.

'Good. Get some rest, Silus, we still have a lot of work to do,' Birchwood said before hanging up.

He sat in silence for a few minutes, outwardly still and calm, while inwardly charged with the excitement and adren-aline from the day's actions. The excitement passed and adrenaline burnt off, leaving him tired. He had just one more task to do before he headed up to bed. His phone buzzed as he opened up a special secure browser on the computer. Paus-ing, Birchwood read the message.

Wright's been called back off holiday for an emergency meeting with the PM and myself on Monday morning, 11:30 at the Nova South building. His security team will be driving him straight there from the airport.

A smile formed on Birchwood's face as he read the message he'd been waiting for. With thoughts of sleep pushed to the back of his mind, Birchwood used the link provided by Montana to access a dark web address with an encrypted contact screen, where he entered his message.

Details of the target and his planned movements are attached. The contract is time sensitive. The target must not be allowed to attend the meeting at the NCSC headquarters on Monday at 11:30am. We are, of course, willing to pay a premium for such short notice.

After sending the message, Birchwood sat staring at the cursor blinking inside the monochrome contact screen, his mind ticking over alternative options if Montana refused to take the contract. Eventually the tiredness returned, and as he didn't expect any kind of immediate response, he leaned forward to turn the monitors off. His finger stopped short, hovering over the off button as the cursor jumped to the bottom of a reply from Montana.

Fee is double. Half now, half on completion, no negotiation.

Birchwood smiled to himself as he typed a response. He would have paid treble.

Agreed. Payment will be with you within the hour.

A message came back quickly.

I will contact you when it's done.

This was followed by a connection termination message. Birchwood paid the upfront fee to the same offshore account as before, then turned the computer off. He stood up and headed out of the room, clicking the light switch off as he went.

'That'll teach you to block me, you fucking asshole. You're a dead man walking,' he muttered, heading up the stairs.

CHAPTER 8

'Mmm, what time did you get in last night?' Nikki said sleepily as Danny rolled over and wrapped his arm around her.

'Just after two,' Danny replied, moving in close to kiss her on the neck.

'Well, at least that's all over with. I didn't know what to think when I saw that pub explosion on the news,' she said, turning over to face him.

'Yeah, we were lucky we left when we did. I've got to go in with Scott this morning to see if I can match this guy to anyone in their database,' Danny replied, forcing a smile to reassure Nikki when a concerned look came immediately back at him.

'Danny! Every time you get involved with that man, people try to kill you,' Nikki said, pulling away from him.

'Yeah, I know. But this time I'm just going to be looking at photos and stuff, trying to identify the man who planted the bomb in the pub. I'll be in the SIS building the whole time. I won't even leave the operations room. Honest. Look at pictures and keep your brother company while he does his computer wizardry. That's it, nothing else.'

There was a tense silence for a few moments until Nikki's face finally softened. Danny took the opportunity to move in and kiss her.

'Oh no you don't, Mr Pearson, you don't get around me that easily,' Nikki said with a smile when Danny moved back.

'No! I guess I'll just have to try harder then,' Danny said, pulling her close as he moved in to kiss her again.

'Oh yeah, that's much harder,' Nikki said softly, kissing him back as he rolled on top of her.

A little while later, Danny sat at the kitchen table drinking his coffee while munching on a piece of toast.

'Scott's here,' came a shout from Nikki as she bounced down the stairs and opened the front door.

'Good morning, sis, is the caveman ready to go?'

'Oi, I heard that,' Danny shouted back.

'Yeah, go on through,' Nikki chuckled.

'Come on, old man, let's go and catch some bad guys,' Scott said, pinching a piece of toast off Danny's plate and walking off with it.

'Alright, alright, I'm coming.' Danny hurriedly finished his remaining piece of toast and gulped down the rest of his coffee to wash it down.

'Whoa, before you two go anywhere, it's just office work, right? No bad guys, guns or dangerous stuff,' Nikki said, giving them a stern look while blocking the doorway.

'I told you we're just helping out. We won't even be leaving the SIS building.'

'Absolutely not, sis. The only killing that will be done is from my superior computer skills,' Scott said with a confident grin.

Danny rolled his eyes and gave Nikki a kiss goodbye before the two of them got into Scott's Porsche 718 Cayman GT4 RS, and rumbled off noisily towards central London.

'When are you going to get a car I can actually sit in

comfortably?' Danny grumbled, squeezed into the low down bucket seat.

'My dear fellow, one doesn't think about comfort when one is driving a car like this. It's an image, a lifestyle choice,' Scott lectured him back.

'It's bloody uncomfortable and I'll need a chiropractor after this,' Danny grumbled.

'Deary me, someone did get out of bed on the wrong side this morning.'

Danny looked across at Scott, the frown dropping off his face to be replaced by a smile.

'Sorry, Scotty boy, working for Simon tends to have that effect on me.'

'Apology accepted. I can drop you back home if you want. I'll tell Simon you've changed your mind.'

'No, I'm not doing this for Simon. This guy who bombed the pub needs to be stopped before he kills more innocent people, so if I can help in any way, I have a moral duty to do so. Also, I'm the only one who knows what he looks like.'

'Ah, well, that's not strictly true,' Scott said, a big grin spreading across his face.

'Scott?'

'All in good time, dear boy. Wait until we get to the SIS building and all will be revealed.'

CHAPTER 9

Professor Silus Montague left his office in the 500-year-old four-storey college building. He headed down the stone staircase and out through a heavy oak door into the courtyard. Walking briskly across the centuries old flagstone path through the centre of the immaculately manicured lawns, Montague left the courtyard through the north exit. After a short walk through the college grounds, he entered the technology department, an ultra modern building funded by a collection of generous sponsors, the most generous of which being Alfred Birchwood. He walked along the corridor heading towards the information and communication technology department, smiling and greeting students and teachers on his way until finally stopping by a door with an ICT.1.23 plaque attached to it. With his hand on the handle, he took a deep breath and fixed a warm smile on his face before pushing it down to enter the classroom full of computers and monitors, all neatly fixed to purpose made desks. Appearing from behind the computer monitors, Rachael, Sebastian and Tobias looked back at him with tired, slightly hungover faces.

'I hope you enjoyed your celebrations last night. You deserve it,' the professor said, smiling warmly, his features resembling those of a proud father, while his thoughts drifted to his long awaited payday and a release from Birchwood's hold over him.

At Birchwood's insistence, Silus had used his talents to handpick and slowly groom this group of misfit geniuses from early teens to the young adults sitting in front of him. A decade earlier, Silus had been grooming boys for a very different purpose. His urges led him to become careless, and a student began to notice his advances towards some of the other boys. He secretly took photos and voice recordings, threatening to expose the professor unless he passed him with honours. That student was Alfred Birchwood. Silus had done as Birchwood demanded, relaxing when Birchwood graduated, leaving the college to enter the business world.

Years later, Alfred Birchwood, CEO of Birchwood Technologies, remotely hacked Montague's laptop, copying some very incriminating media content - pictures and videos Montague shared with a select group of like-minded friends, some of which mixed in powerful circles. Faced with public humiliation, losing his position as dean of the college and prosecution, Silus agreed once more to do as Birchwood demanded.

'Tobias, are you alright this morning?' said Montague, looking at Tobias as he twitched and looked over at Sebastian.

'What about the ones who died in the pub explosion?'

'Give it a rest, Tobias, we went through all this last night. Fucking deal with it,' Sebastian said, cutting Tobias dead, dominating him as always.

'Y-yes Professor, I'm fine,' Tobias said in a quiet voice, looking away from Sebastian towards Montague, still avoiding eye contact.

'The deaths are regrettable and we all feel for their families, but we needed the establishment to sit up and take notice. You should be proud of yourselves. Yesterday you took the first step in giving yourselves and an entire generation hope, hope that someone cares more about having a future than money, hope that there are people willing to stand and fight for them. Breaking the establishment was never going to be easy, you are pioneers, outcasts in the short term, heroes and saviours in the long term,' Montague said, taking in the adoration of the students as they looked back at him, captivated by every word he spoke.

'Hell yeah. I take it you've seen the media and socials,' said Sebastian excitedly, with Rachael grinning beside him.

'Yes I have, Sebastian, far right members of Extinction Rebellion, Just Stop Oil and even Greenpeace are all showing their support for Genesis UK. It's a wonderful start. But we cannot get too carried away. We still have a long way to go.'

'When are we going to meet our benefactor, Professor?' Sebastian continued, power drunk on their success.

Tobias stood next to them. He smiled and nodded with them, but the anxiety never really left his face.

'Soon, Sebastian, soon. Our benefactor is working from within the government. If he reveals himself before we have the support we need to take power, Genesis UK will be destroyed and he will be sent to prison. He's risking everything to support us. You just need to be patient. Now, enough about that. Do you have everything set for this morning's follow up?'

'Yeah, Tob's got a back door open and ready to go,' said Sebastian, taking control as usual.

'And you've got your digital footprint covered?' Montague said, his stern manner and stare cutting through Sebastian's over confidence.

'Yes, Professor, we took every precaution,' Rachael cut in, looking to the other two for confirmation.

'Yes, we're covered,' said Tobias, nodding beside him.

'Very good. I'll leave you to it then. Oh, and I'm very proud of all of you,' Montague said, watching the students lap up his praise, the words filling the empty void left by their emotionally unattached parents.

CHAPTER 10

cott stopped at the lights with Vauxhall Bridge ahead of them, and the SIS building just visible on the other side of the Thames.

'So Daniel, what's the plan now you're married to my sister? Am I going to hear the pitter patter of tiny little feet and the call of Uncle Scott any time soon?'

'Er, what, I, er,' Danny stammered, the question taking him by surprise.

'Look, I know the memory of losing Sarah and your son, Timothy, will always be painful, but that was a long time ago. You have a new wife and the clock's ticking, old man.'

'What's brought this on, Scott? Has Nikki said something?' Danny said.

'No, no, it's just a feeling. You've seen how she is with your brother's children,' Scott said, pulling away as the lights turned green.

'Mmm, yeah, I know,' Danny said, looking out of the side window as he thought about what Scott had said. 'Shit, floor it, Scott,' Danny shouted, whipping around to shoot his hand across and push down hard on Scott's right knee. Jerking at the force of Danny's grip, Scott's foot kicked down on the accelerator, making the powerful Porsche take off across the junction. A lorry locked up its wheels as it slid into the junction from the left-hand side before passing inches from the back of the Porsche. It crossed the junction and destroyed a black cab as it came off the junction on the opposite side. More cars piled in from all directions, turning the junction into a twisted metal mess.

'What the hell's going on?' Scott said, slowing down when Danny released his knee to look at the junction in the rear-view mirror.

'Sorry, the lights were all green,' Danny said, twisting in his seat to look behind them.

'Yes, I know. That's why I drove off,' said Scott, confused.

'No, mate, you don't understand. All the lights were green on both sides.'

'Good god, how the hell did that happen? Well, at least the Porsche is alright. Do you have any idea how much it costs to fix a dent in one of these things? Oh, hang on, what's happening up ahead?' Scott said, slowing for a queue of stationary traffic at the junction next to the SIS building on the far side of the bridge.

As they got closer, Danny could see a mass of crashed and wedged cars filling the yellow boxed area in the middle of the junction, with no way of getting out as more cars piled in behind them.

'Quick, bump over the curb onto the cycle path, Scott. It's the only way we're going to get to the building's entrance around the corner,' said Danny, pointing to the wide tarmac cycle path running alongside the pavement.

'What? With these low-profile tyres and alloys? I don't think so,' Scott said, pulling to a stop behind the line of cars.

'Suit yourself, Scotty boy. I'll get out and walk, mate. You'll probably still be here when I'm ready to go home,' Danny said, reaching for the door release to get out.

'Argh, ok, alright, here we go,' grumbled Scott, wincing

when the car made a scraping sound as he bumped over the kerb.

They bumped down the other side and drove at a crawl around the corner, ignoring shouts and a two-fingered salute from an angry cyclist coming the other way. Just as they pulled up to the SIS building's security gate, Danny looked back to see all the lights at the junction behind them showing green, just like the ones before the bridge. After showing their passes, they parked up in the building's underground car park and made their way through security before heading up to the sixth floor operations room. They entered the room to a hive of activity. Camera feeds of the traffic chaos from all across London filled the screens. Naturally curious, Scott wandered over to take a closer look.

Danny hung back, taking in the scene until a familiar voice came from behind him.

'Well, it's got to be bad if they've called you in.'

He turned to see a friend he hadn't seen for a few years.

'John, good to see you, man. You're looking good,' Danny replied, shaking John Ball's hand.

'Don't lie to me mate, I look old and fat,' John said with a chuckle.

'So what are you up to these days, still doing field work?' Danny said, ignoring the old and fat comment.

'Every now and again. I spend most of my time chained to a desk these days. Speaking of which, here comes the boss, so I'd better get back at it,' John said, spotting Edward Jenkins heading their way.

'Ok mate, I'll catch up with you later,' Danny said, letting him go as the Chief of the Secret Intelligence Service, Edward Jenkins, came over to greet him.

'Morning Edward, no Simon this morning?' Danny said.

'No, in light of recent events, the PM's called him in to attend an urgent COBR meeting. He should be here later on.'

'So what do you want me to do?'

'Not too much at the moment. The whole of London's in chaos with the attack on the Transport for London traffic systems. Most of my staff are stuck somewhere and half the people you see here are stragglers from the night shift, covering until they arrive. Look, why don't you grab yourself a coffee while I try to get some normality back to the office,' Edward said, pointing towards a small kitchenette with coffee machines, fridge and a microwave.

As Danny headed for the coffee machine, his eyes fell on one of the incident whiteboards, with the Red Lion bombing at the top and a string of photographs with names beside them and arrows pointing to jobs and known colleagues.

'What's that?' he said, turning back to Edward.

'That's one theory we're not ruling out. The possibility that the actual targets for the Red Lion bombing were the Minister for technology, Christian Flowers and a political advisor and cyber security expert, James Howman, and Colin Trowbridge, a designer and supplier of the Ministry of Defence IT systems.'

'I've seen them before,' Danny said, frowning.

'Where?'

'In the pub before the explosion, Scott was talking to them when I arrived.'

'Really? It was lucky you two left when you did,' said Edward, the two of them turning to look across the room at Scott.

'You don't think Scott was a target?' said Danny, thinking out loud.

'I wouldn't have thought so. Genesis UK is all about attacking the establishment and Scott's not known for any political ties.'

CHAPTER 11

After leaving the Airbnb early Oliver Johnson took an underground train to Victoria, only to discover the traffic chaos caused by Genesis's latest attack as he exited Victoria station. He stood outside in the morning sun, his baseball cap pulled down so its peak almost touched the top of his sunglasses. The sandy coloured wig he wore underneath the cap curled up as it hit the top of his shoulders, while a set of prosthetic teeth altered the shape of his mouth, pushing his cheeks out to give his face a more rounded appearance. He looked beyond the stationary buses, blocked from leaving their depot outside Victoria station by Genesis UK's traffic chaos.

Zoning out the throng of revving engines, horns and angry, impatient drivers, Johnson focused on the tall, wedge-shaped metal and glass office block towering above a Victorian three-storey parade of shops, restaurants and cafes on the far side of the bus depot. A motorbike backfiring as the rider wound it up to snake between the stationary traffic broke his concentration.

Old bullet wounds in his shoulder and side screamed with

a phantom pain made real years after healing. An unwelcome memory replayed in his head, his hands tied behind his back while he knelt in his own piss in a stinking basement. Two men from a splinter cell group of Al Qaeda punched and kicked him, working themselves up, ready to chop his head off with a two-foot-long machete. Fighting against fear and panic, he knew this was his last chance to do something or accept his fate. Watching their movements through swollen eyes, Johnson launched himself up off his knees, whipping his head to one side as he planted his boots firmly on the dirt floor.

The hard part of his skull cracked into the face of the man with the machete. Cartilage and bone collapsed as the man went down with blood flowing out of his nose. Charged up on self preservation, rage and adrenaline, Johnson shoulder-charged the second man, smacking his back into the wall of the basement, his shoulder continuing to drive into the man's chest, crushing the air out of him until his ribs cracked. When Johnson stepped back, the man fell to the floor with panic in his eyes. As he sucked in an excruciatingly painful breath of air to shout for help, Johnson kicked out, driving the heel of his boot into the man's throat, crushing his Adam's apple into his windpipe. The man grabbed his throat, his eyes wide, unable to breathe or make a noise. Leaving him rolling about on the floor, Johnson dropped into a crouch with his back to the unconscious man he'd headbutted.

Feeling around with his hands tied behind his back, his fingers found the handle of the machete. With an awkward bit of manipulation, he held it so the blade pointed upwards and rubbed the razor-sharp edge on his bindings until they frayed enough to snap. Free at last, he breathed steadily and moved out of the basement, working his way up the bare concrete steps towards the ground floor.

As he neared the top, a robed man walked into view. Their

eyes met. Surprise, fear, then rage flashed across the man's face as he pulled a Sig handgun from his belt. Johnson lunged forward, driving the man into the bare concrete block shell of a room by plunging the blade of the machete into his abdomen. When it was ten inches in, Johnson jerked his hands down and thrust the machete upwards under the rib cage and into his heart.

Muzzle flashes lit up the room as the dying terrorist jerked the trigger, the bullets hitting Johnson like a sledgehammer, forcing him to let go of the machete as they knocked him backwards until he fell out of a glassless window. Dazed and confused, Johnson rolled onto his front and crawled through thorny bushes into a dry, rocky ditch. Breathing heavily until the pain subsided enough to move, Johnson got to his knees and then to his feet and staggered away across the barren landscape.

With a trickle of cold sweat rolling down his cheek, Johnson pushed the image and emotion down deep and concentrated on the contract. He walked around to the front of the parade of shops to take his first clear look at the Nova South building, home of the National Cyber Security Centre, and the location his target would arrive at for his meeting at 11:30am on Monday morning.

Security measures were already being stepped up. A HIAB lorry was using its crane to lower concrete barriers on one side of the road to form a drop-off zone, protection from anyone attempting to ram the building or plant a car bomb outside the entrance. Two armed officers stood just outside the entrance doors with two more visible through the glass as they stood by the security desk in reception. Johnson had expected this, the bombing on the pub and Genesis UK's cyber attack had put the capital's terrorism threat to a level 5, critical alert status, meaning an attack was likely in the near future.

Johnson walked past the front of the building on the opposite side of the road, crossing it to head down a wide pedestrian walkway with trees, plants, and benches dotted down the middle. It ran down the side of the Nova South building, all the way down to Nova North, a matching wedge-shaped building set behind it. He sat on the bench nearest the front of the Nova South building, taking in every detail of the walkway. Turning his head, Johnson looked through the floor-to-ceiling glass panels at the side of the building, giving him a view into the foyer and security check area. Time was short and options limited. He would have preferred a long distance sniper shot, but the surrounding buildings with the bus depot and Victoria station behind them didn't offer any line of sight of the entrance as cars dropped people off for the meeting. Access to the building itself would be very difficult with such short notice, and intercepting his target as he drove from the airport to the meeting would require multiple vehicles and a three or four-man team. No, it would have to be here when the target left his vehicle to go inside.

After a while, Johnson got up and walked casually away from the building. He entered a small park to escape the noise of the still gridlocked traffic. Taking a seat, he tapped a list of items into a message on his phone before dialing a number from memory into his phone and pressing call.

'It's Montana. I'm going to send you a list of items I require,' Johnson said, hitting send on the list when he'd finished.

There was a pause while the contact read the list.

'Ok, no problem.'

'I have to have them by Saturday. Is that going to be a problem?'

There was another pause.

'No problem. It will cost a lot more for such short notice,' the man on the other end said bluntly.

'Understood. By Saturday,' Johnson replied, hanging up straight afterwards.

He looked at the traffic chaos and back across at Victoria station, deciding to walk back to the apartment instead of taking the Tube.

CHAPTER 12

Turning away from the large screens, Scott spotted a group of computer techs huddled around two operatives as they worked frantically on their computer terminals. He walked over and stood behind them, listening as they all talked over each other with a host of different opinions on the latest hack into London's traffic signal system, managed by Transport for London. As he stood watching, the room fell into silence as everyone's phones pinged simultaneously with an incoming message.

A new dawn is breaking. They are not in control, we are. Genesis UK is hope. Genesis UK will give you a future.

'Mmm, persistent little buggers, aren't they? May I take a look?' Scott said with a cheery smile.

Turning to see the renowned Scott Miller standing behind them, they stepped aside and let him through.

'Here, Mr Miller, take my seat,' the operative at the desk said, getting up to offer it to Scott.

'Thank you, my good man. Now, do we have a link into the traffic signal systems?'

'Yes sir, Transport for London alerted us and the NCSC as soon as the system was hacked. We have Jim Platt, a senior technician for Transport for London and Gregory Matel from NCSC, live on speakerphone.'

'The National Cyber Security Centre, well, we must be in good hands then. Good morning, gentlemen, how's it going?' Scott said a little sarcastically.

He placed his laptop bag on the floor and sat down, taking over the keyboard and mouse to scroll through pages of program code.

'It's not going. We can't reboot the system. They've planted a virus making the program unresponsive. If we pull the plug, we might not get it up and running again,' came Jim's rather stressed voice over the speakerphone.

'Yes, quite. You don't mind if I have a little poke around, do you?' Scott said, already inside the program before Jim could answer.

'Hang on there, NCSC has this situation fully under control. Just who the hell am I talking to?'

'My name is Scott Miller, Mr Matel, and I'm sure you and Mr Platt are wonderfully competent at your jobs, but I was designing systems more complicated than this one when I was still at school,' Scott answered with a fair amount of smugness.

'Listen, Mr Miller, you don't have authority. I'll have to speak to my bosses,' said Jim Platt, worried at the intrusion.

'I'm ordering you not to interfere. We have this under control,' came Mr Matel's angry voice over the speaker.

'There you go, all done. It was a fairly simple piece of looping software to convince the system that the signal for red light was actually activating the green light. I'm surprised you didn't spot it straight away. Now, I suggest you get together and have a little discussion about security and fire-wall measures,' Scott said, interrupting Mr Platt and Mr Matel as he corrected the hack by Genesis.

'Done! What? You can't be... Let me... Er, yeah, system's back online and everything's working as it should. But how?'

'Thank you very much. You may have your chair back now. Gentlemen,' Scott said, ignoring the two men on speakerphone as he got up and walked away from the techies, heading over to Danny and Edward.

'So you have no leads on this character?' Danny said, both of them looking at an incident board at the side of the room.

There was a description of the man Danny had chased with arrows going out to lots of unanswered questions. Where did he come from? The only answered question was how did he pay for his Tube journey? It was a contactless transaction made with a stolen bank card. They didn't know where he went as the card wasn't used to tap out of any station.

'Sorry, nothing, I've got a team checking hotels in the Greater London area, but with the amount and vague description, I don't hold much luck.'

'I might be able to help you there,' said Scott, patting his laptop bag.

'Go on, Scott,' said Edward.

'Well, if you'll allow me some space and access to your monitors I'll show you,' Scott said, looking around for a free desk.

'Of course. Simpkins, clear a space for Mr Miller and give him access to the displays please,' Edward said, shouting across to one of his men at the front of the room.

A desk was cleared in double time, allowing Scott to set up his laptop and attach it to MI6's network and bank of display screens.

'So, what have you got, Scotty boy?' said Danny, watching Scott tap furiously away at the keyboard.

'Any second now, dear boy, and voila,' said Scott, hitting the enter key before looking up at the screens as they burst into life.

A hundred or more pictures and videos taken from a whole host of social media posts from around Big Ben, Parliament, Westminster Abbey and Westminster Bridge covered the displays. One by one, the pieces of a man in the background of each post became shaded and detached themselves from the posts and moved to a central screen. Bits of head, body, arms, and legs, from all angles, spun, resized and joined together, Scott's program adjusting the shading and filling in the missing pieces until it formed a three-dimensional image of the man Danny had chased.

'That's him, exactly him in every detail,' Danny said, amazed at how clear Scott's reconstruction was.

'I had my computers running through social media all night looking for matching locations, or images of the area posted over the last twenty-four hours, then I had them search for any pieces matching our man's description, and there you are. I can also tell you that by analysing scalable background images and landmarks, our man is approximately one hundred and eighty-two centimetres, that's six feet tall to you, Daniel, and weighs around one hundred and three kilos.'

'Brilliant work, Scott, I'll get this out to all our agents. Even if he's disguised, it's a good start,' said Edward.

'That's not all. My search for media discovered that our man didn't take a Tube train anywhere. He doubled back on himself and exited the station at Westminster Pier, before crossing Westminster Bridge on foot and heading along the Thames path. I had a couple of hits with him in the background as people took photos of the London Eye, but lost the trail as he moved away from the popular tourist areas to the back streets around Waterloo train station,' Scott finished, leaning back in the chair and smiling like a Cheshire Cat.

'Ok, great,' Edward said, turning to address the room. 'Listen up, people, we have pictures and a last known sighting of our bomber. I want every available agent checking shops, hotels, bed and breakfasts, cafes and restaurants within a mile of the London Eye. Show the pictures of that man to everyone. We suspect he was in disguise. He'll have wanted to change as soon as possible. Search alleyways, bins, anywhere he could have ditched his clothing and that red bag. Keep in radio contact. You get anything, you call it in.'

Edward finished addressing the room and called over to John Ball, 'John, get onto the Met and tell them we need some police officers to help with the search.'

'Yes sir,' replied John, immediately picking up a phone.

'Let's hustle, people, we need to get on this while the lead is hot,' shouted Edward, the atmosphere in the room changing as it burst into a thrum of urgent activity.

'Hey, Edward, do you mind if I tag along? I'll only get in the way here,' Danny said, itching to get involved.

'Yes, but only as an observer. You see anything, you call it in, ok? You can go with John as soon as he's off the phone. It'll be quicker on foot. Traffic's going to take hours to clear after Genesis's little stunt.'

'Ok, no problem. I'll catch up with you both later,' Danny said to Scott and Edward before heading over to John, still on the phone to the Commissioner of the Metropolitan Police.

CHAPTER 13

By the time Danny and John got to the London Eye with four other MI6 agents, six uniform officers from the Metropolitan Police force had arrived to help. John handed printouts of Scott's computer generated image of the bomber around and divided them into pairs, sending them off into different areas on either side of Waterloo station.

'So what do we do?' Danny said when they'd all gone.

'We'll start around here. Scott said he came this way, so we'll work our way along the river and through the park. Ask all the street sellers and entertainers if they've seen him.'

'Ok, you're the boss.'

An hour passed and two of Edward's agents stepped out of Gail's Bakery at the top of Chicheley Street after another blank look and shrug from the staff at the picture of the bomber.

'You know this is pointless, don't you?' one of them said as they both looked up and down York Road trying to decide who to ask next.

'Yep, who's going to remember some random guy from

yesterday?' the older agent said, holding up the picture in front of him.

'I remember that guy,' came a slurred voice from behind them.

They turned slowly to see a homeless man sitting on the bench, a rolled-up sleeping bag and a carrier bag holding his worldly belongings on one side and a four-pack of cheap beer on the other. He smiled to reveal a couple of peg-like teeth in his mouth.

'You've seen this guy?' The older agent said, pointing at the picture doubtfully.

'Yes sir, yesterday morning. He stopped and gave me a twenty-pound note. He's a Yank, a tourist I guess. He told me to get some breakfast with it. God bless America.'

The two agents looked at each other in disbelief.

'Do you know where he went?'

'Nope,' he replied, his filthy hands curling around a beer can to show chipped nails black with the filth of the streets wedged under them as he gulped the alcoholic liquid down.

'Come on, we're not going to get anything more here,' the younger agent said.

'But I know where he came from,' he said as the agents started to walk away.

They turned back to see a devious twinkle in the drunk's bloodshot eyes.

'Where?' the older agent said, tiring of the homeless man's rambling.

'I can see you fine young fellas want him badly. Information like that's gotta to be worth something, I guess,' he said, unfolding his other hand to show them a filthy, sweaty palm.

'You'd better not be pissing us about, old man,' the older agent said, pulling a ten pound note from his wallet to place it in the homeless guy's hand, releasing it without touching his filthy flesh.

'Now I'm not sure who's pissing who about,' the old man said, looking disapprovingly at the ten pound note.

Begrudgingly, the older agent pulled another ten pound note out and placed it in his hand, which immediately folded around the money and shoved it quickly into his jacket pocket.

'He came out of that building over there,' the old man said, pointing to the building next door to a Premier Inn hotel across the road.

'The office building?'

'No, dumbass, the door around the side, the one for the apartments at the top.'

They left him and crossed over to the entrance to the foyer. Pushing the door open, they went inside and checked out the mailboxes fitted to the wall opposite the lift and stairs.

'Let's call it in.'

'Ok,' the older agent said, getting his radio out of his pocket.

'Agent Sinclair to control, over.'

'Go ahead, Sinclair.'

'We've had a confirmed sighting of the suspect leaving the entrance to five apartments located above the offices of 75-79 York Road. Our witness spoke to the suspect, who is believed to be an American.'

'Hold on, Sinclair.'

There was a brief pause before Edward's voice came over the radio.

'Hold your position. We're running a check on the apartments now.'

Five minutes away, Danny and John heard the radio chatter.

'That's not far from here, let's check it out,' said Danny, already changing direction towards York Road.

'Wait, Danny, you stay with me. You're only supposed to

be an observer. We do this by the book, right?' replied John, trying to catch Danny up.

'Yeah, yeah, by the book. Come on, let's go,' Danny said over his shoulder.

Back in the foyer, the two agents looked at each other then at the lift opposite.

'Couldn't do any harm to just go up and have a look around,' the younger one said.

His partner thought for a second, then nodded, pressing the button and entering the lift. They exited onto a corridor on the top floor and walked along its length, taking care not to make any sound. There were three doors to apartments facing the front of the building and two doors to apartments facing the rear. Agent Sinclair checked the numbered door lock before gently placing his ear to the door of the apartment at the end of the corridor, listening for any signs of life. When he got none, he shook his head to his partner, and they moved to the next apartment door to listen again. When he got to the third apartment, his radio burst into life, making him jump and scramble to turn the volume down.

'Control to Sinclair, come in.'

'Go ahead, control,' Sinclair said in a hushed voice as he stepped away from the door.

'The apartments are owned by a property company and rented out through the Airbnb website. Numbers four and five are empty. The people renting apartments two and three have checked out, a Chinese couple on holiday and a repeat booking for a Dr Kayode from Nigeria. Apartment 1 has an online booking to a Mr Alan Thomas. His contact details, email and name do not match up through the system. The property company has given us the door code, it's 3781Y. Other agents are on their way. Wait until they arrive, then proceed with extreme caution.'

Agent Sinclair put his finger to his lips then pointed to his eyes and the door of apartment one. While he pulled the gun from his shoulder holster, his younger partner did the same, following closely behind him. Treading carefully, he put his ear to the apartment door and listened for what felt like ages. He eventually took his ear off the door and shook his head to his partner.

'I don't think anyone's there.'

'Where's the other agents?' his partner said, looking back at the lift and stairs.

'Fuck it, let's go in,' Sinclair said, looking at the number lock in front of him.

His partner nodded in agreement, taking a step back to put his gun up in front of him, covering over Sinclair's shoulder as he pressed the entry code into the lock.

CHAPTER 14

After a leisurely walk through central London, Johnson joined York Road a hundred metres or so from the apartment. He walked along, picking out anyone in the crowd of tourists and workers that caught his eye, before trusting his instincts to discount them as a potential threat. He noticed the homeless drunk he'd given money to the day before, still sitting on the same bench, but this time he had a fresh bottle of cheap spirit gripped tightly in his grimy hands as he rambled nonsensically to the tourists giving him a wide berth. Continuing on his way, Johnson walked on the opposite side of the road to the building with his apartment on top. He didn't look directly in its direction, opting instead to pull in as much sensory information in his peripheral vision as he could. No alarm bells rang. He walked another thirty metres further on before crossing the road and heading back towards the apartment. After a final scan of his surroundings, Johnson entered the building. Ignoring the lift, he headed up the stairs, his feet moving at a fast pace while the soles of his trainers hit the steps so lightly they barely made a sound. He turned on the final landing, freezing as he placed a foot on the first step. The colours of the corridor wall lightened as he looked through the glass in the fire door up ahead. Natural sunlight from one of the apartment doors being opened washed the soft LED lighting of the corridors spot lights out. Johnson moved up to get a better look. As he did, the tiny camera in his apartment sent a motion trigger alert to the phone in his pocket. Pulling it out, he watched two agents entering the living room. Very calmly, Johnson started backing down the stairs. He turned and quickened his pace, only making it down one floor when voices from somewhere below stopped him.

'John Ball to Agent Sinclair. We are at the location now. Come in, Sinclair.'

'Sinclair to Ball, we have entered the apartment. There is no sign of the suspect. Come on up.'

Johnson's face went taut, the muscles in his cheeks tensed as he clenched his teeth. He turned and moved up the stairs, putting both hands under his jacket to pull out two punch knives from leather sheaths worn on the inside of the waistband of his jeans. With the T-shaped handles held in his fists, and the five centimetre razor-sharp blades sticking out like large arrowheads between his middle fingers, Johnson moved up to the fire door at the top of the stairs. He took a few deep breaths, tensing his muscles as he mentally prepared himself, then pulled the fire door open. Exploding into action, he sprinted towards the open apartment door.

Inside, Sinclair turned, expecting to see Agent Ball instead of Johnson hurtling towards him. By the time he raised his gun, Johnson was upon him, swiping the gun aside with his left arm as Sinclair pulled the trigger, while simultaneously punching the blade between the fingers on his right hand repeatedly into Sinclair's torso. The shock and sharpness of the blade stopped Sinclair from feeling any pain. He shook as Johnson continued to punch a blisteringly fast combination of stabs to his torso, working him like a punchbag. Sinclair collapsed, his mouth opening and closing, the puncture wounds deflating his lungs, denying him from making a sound. He looked down, his eyes widening in horror at the river of blood flowing out of his chest. Johnson had already gone. Spinning away, he bolted across the lounge as Sinclair's partner rushed out of the bedroom with his gun up ahead of him. Watching the agent's every move, Johnson swung his left arm out and slashed the agent across his wrist, cutting tendons and the radial artery. As the gun dropped to the floor and blood sprayed from his wrist, Johnson punched and dragged the blade in his right hand across the agent's neck, dropping him as a second fountain of arterial blood shot up the wall. Darting into the bedroom, Johnson tucked the punch knives back into their sheaths, grabbed a pre-packed rucksack with a few clothes, fake passports, bank cards, money, mobile phones, and a silenced Beretta inside. He threw it onto his back while running back into the lounge to get his laptop.

'Gunshot,' Danny shouted, taking off up the stairs three at a time.

'Danny, wait,' John called after him, distracted for a second by agonising groans coming over the radio. 'Sinclair. Come in, Sinclair.'

Going for speed over caution, Danny charged into the apartment, pulling to a dead stop at the sight of Sinclair's body on the floor. A dining table sat in front of him with a laptop on top. On the far side of the table, standing in front of the glass doors with views of the London Eye beyond, was the man he'd chased from the Red Lion pub. The hair under his baseball cap was a different length and colour and his eyes, now brown, flicked from Danny to the laptop, but it was definitely the same man. John blundering into the apartment behind Danny with his gun in his hand, broke the stalemate. Johnson turned and pulled the glass door open, darting through as Danny skirted the table to give chase. Johnson hopped up onto the stainless steel and glass panelled railing that ran around the terrace before jumping up and pulling himself onto the overhanging flat roof above them. Danny wasted no time. He leapt up to place his feet on the railing, twisting his body around with a hundred-foot sheer drop beneath him to jump up, pulling himself onto the flat roof in one smooth motion. Johnson was still ahead of him, weaving in and out of the various vents, ducting and air-conditioning units as he sprinted for the far corner of the roof.

As Danny ran after him, Johnson reached the edge of the building, bent down and threw a doubled-up climber's rope off the edge. Wrapping the rope between his legs and around his lower back, Johnson leaned out over the edge, his eyes staring coldly at Danny as he pushed off and disappeared out of sight. Seconds later, Danny reached the edge and looked over. Johnson was halfway down, kicking off the wall while feeding the rope out in a fast South African rappel.

There was nothing Danny could do to stop him, the rope was firmly tied around some pipework, and he didn't have a knife to cut it. Within ten seconds, Johnson's feet touched the floor. He shook off the ropes and looked up. Their eyes locked for the briefest moment before he turned and ran out of sight around the back of the Premier Inn hotel next door.

Turning away, Danny headed across the roof back to the apartment. He hopped down onto the railing, then onto the terrace. A few streets away, Johnson ditched the baseball cap, wig and his blood splattered jacket into the nearest bin. Still moving fast, he pulled a lightweight jacket from his go bag and slipped it on, flipping its hood up before merging with the crowd to vanish from sight. As he headed away from the area, he scrolled through his phone and opened a web page. When the status said connected, he hit a button and watched the word "Armed" display in red letters. Back up at the apartment, Danny stepped into the lounge to see John with his hand on the laptop, ready to open the lid.

'Stop, John, don't,' was all Danny could say before John

lifted the lid and disappeared inside a ball of flame and debris as the laptop exploded.

The blast wave punched into Danny's chest knocking him off his feet as the glass doors on either side of him blew out, the tiny fragments twinkling in the air around him as he flew backwards across the terrace, cracking his head and back into the railing on the far side. With his ears ringing, Danny's concussed brain registered the destruction inside the smoking apartment. He rolled over onto his front, taking several deep breaths before dragging himself onto his knees, finally pulling himself upright using the stainless steel railing. A hand touching his back made him whip around with his fist raised, only to see one of Edward's agents standing behind him. A couple of Metropolitan Police officers moved around in the background, putting out bits of smouldering furniture with a fire extinguisher from the corridor.

'Whoa, it's ok, take it easy.'

Putting his hand down, Danny leaned on the railing to get his breath back and wait for the ringing in his ears to stop.

'John,' he said, looking into the wrecked apartment.

The agent's face fell as he shook his head.

CHAPTER 15

Across the city, Johnson headed for Oxford Street getting supplies from a chemist before entering a sports shop to get a change of clothes. When he came out, he walked straight into the nearest McDonald's restaurant and headed for the toilets. He locked himself inside a cubicle and hooked his shopping bag on the back of the door. Wincing in pain, he slid the rucksack off his back and pulled his lightweight jacket off to reveal bloodstained lines running around his back in the T-shirt underneath. Carefully, Johnson pulled the T-shirt up, its cotton material tearing at the skin as he peeled it free, slipping it up and over his head. After checking the rope burns from the rapid rappel off the apartment roof without a harness, Johnson took the dressings he'd purchased from the chemist out of the shopping bag and patched himself up.

Happy with the patch-up job, he pulled on a new T-shirt, hooded jumper and trainers before placing a new baseball cap and sunglasses on his head. He put the old clothes and trainers into the carrier bag from the sports shop and left McDonald's. Disposing of the carrier bag of clothes in the waste bin outside, Johnson headed for the nearest underground station. He changed lines at Baker Street and emerged from the underground platforms into the main station at Paddington.

Even with some distance between the apartment and here, Johnson didn't allow himself to relax. He hung back to one side of the underground exit, letting the other commuters go past while he scanned the station from right to left, his eyes flicking around the sea of moving bodies for anything out of place: men hanging around awkwardly; focused, serious faces looking his way; heads turning as eyes searched entrances and exits. When he didn't see any, he walked casually into the station, just like a thousand other daytrippers going about their business with no care what anyone else was doing. He headed for the far corner of the station, walking past a left luggage and baggage storage depot to a nearby coffee and sandwich stall. He ordered an espresso and took a few paces away, tilting his head up a little to look like he was studying the arrival and departure screens.

Behind the sunglasses, Johnson continued to search the station for signs he'd been compromised. By the time he'd finished his drink, he was satisfied no one was tailing him and headed into the left luggage depot. He showed his receipt slip to the man behind the counter who fetched a small suitcase from the secure storage out back. Johnson thanked him and left, pushing his way across the station to look at the departure screen.

The Heathrow Airport express train was leaving in twenty minutes. He thought about how close he'd come to being captured, and about the man who chased him from the pub bombing nearly getting him for a second time. In twenty minutes, he could be away. He could book the next available flight out of the country and be sleeping soundly in a hotel somewhere a long way from here, safe. Then he thought about the contract. He'd already been paid half the money. If he backed out now, his reputation would be ruined. More dangerous than his reputation was the trust that would be broken. This client was powerful, with deep pockets. What's to say he wouldn't put a hit out on him if he backed out?

Pulling the phone from his pocket, Johnson searched the area for Airbnb accommodation, settling on a house a couple of miles away in Camden Town. The keys were in a combination lockbox mounted by the front door, alleviating the need to meet and be seen by the owner or letting agent. Johnson booked it under one of his other identities, then headed back to the underground to catch the next train to Camden.

CHAPTER 16

'So how was your day?' Danny said, trying to keep the egg-sized lump on the back of his head from tapping against the headrest as Scott changed gear in the Porsche.

'Considerably less exciting than yours by the sounds of it. I spent most of the day analysing data, trying to trace this Genesis UK lot,' Scott said, giving the accelerator a tap, so Danny's head bounced painfully on the headrest.

'Ouch, pack it in. You're like a bloody child,' Danny grumbled, throwing Scott a sideways look.

'Sorry, old man, I just couldn't resist. Oh, I nearly forgot, in light of the deaths of the Minister for Technology, his political advisor and my good friend Colin Trowbridge in that dreadful pub bombing, I've been asked if I would attend an emergency meeting with the bigwigs at the National Cyber Security Centre on Monday to offer my expert assistance.'

'The NCSC, part of GCHQ, haven't they got plenty of experts of their own?' Danny said, leaning forward in his seat in case Scott put his foot down again.

'Yes, plenty of experts in plenty of individual fields, but not as many as one would think who have the knowledge to deal with these kinds of sophisticated attacks. Colin was a leader in this field, now he's dead. There was another who used to work at the NCSC. Er, what was his name? Mrozinski, I think, Polish gentleman, he was very good. Died in some sort of traffic accident a few months back. So no, there's not too many of us about.'

'Mrozinski died a few months ago?' Danny said, looking directly at Scott.

'Yes, he was hit by a delivery truck, I think.'

'And that doesn't seem odd to you, considering what's been going on the last couple of days?'

'Well, yes, when you put it like that, it does seem like a bit too much of a coincidence. Should I be worried?' Scott said, pulling over outside Danny's house.

'I wouldn't have thought so. Nobody outside of MI6 knows that you're looking at this. I'll tell you what, I'll come along on Monday and hang about until you've finished your little meeting and then we can go for a spot of lunch,' Danny said, giving Scott a reassuring grin.

'That sounds like a splendid idea.'

'Anyway, the only one that should be worried is me, when your sister sees the state I'm in,' said Danny with dirt and rips in his clothes and a patch of singed hair sticking straight up at the front of his head.

'Well, good luck with that one. I'll pick you up first thing Monday morning,' Scott said as Danny got out.

Danny waved him off and walked to his front door, sliding the key in carefully before gently opening it and slipping inside, closing the door silently behind him. He could hear the radio through the partly open kitchen door and the soft rumble of the kettle boiling behind it.

'Hi honey, I'm just going to have a shower and change of clothes before dinner, ok?' he shouted, thinking it would be easier to downplay the day's excitement when he was showered and wearing clean clothes.

With his feet already climbing the stairs before she had a chance to answer, Danny looked away from the kitchen door to the top of the stairs only to find Nikki standing on the landing looking down at him, her arms crossed and a look of worried annoyance on her face.

'Eh, hello love, you had a good day?' he said, putting on his best cheeky grin.

'Don't give me, hello love. No danger,' you said. 'I'll just be looking at photos,' you said. 'I won't leave MI6's office,' you said.

'Ah, yeah, I know, but it wasn't my fault. We were just walking about showing Scott's mock-up picture of the guy who bombed the pub, and the next thing I knew we ran straight into him. He legged it and got away. When I returned to his apartment an old friend of mine hit a booby trap. It blew him and the whole bloody apartment up,' Danny said, sadness written all over his face, immediately realising he might have over shared on the explosion bit.

'What? Dead! Explosion!' she gasped.

'Do you mind if we don't talk about it?' Danny said, pausing before adding. 'It doesn't matter now. They've got photofits of the guy now, so they don't need me anymore.' Danny reached the top of the stairs and put his arms around Nikki, emotionally drained.

'Good,' she said, her face eventually softening as she placed her arms around the back of his neck.

'See, I'm fine, everything is working as it should,' he said, looking down, then up, forcing a grin onto his face while pinching her bum and pulling her close to kiss her.

When they parted, Nikki pushed him away. 'Are you sure you're ok?'

'Not really, but I will be,' Danny answered, his face dropping at the thought of the death of his friend.

'Ok, you go and have a shower while I fix you a drink. You smell like a bonfire.'

CHAPTER 17

'Good shot, sir,' said the young Cambridge Country Club caddie, paid to assist Alfred Birchwood during his round of golf.

Birchwood continued to face forward, watching as his ball bounced and rolled until it finished up three metres from the flag. He bent down and picked up his tee, then turned and handed the 2-wood to the caddie, waiting until he'd taken it from him before speaking.

'Take your tongue out of my arse and keep quiet, boy, and I might decide not to have you fired when we're done.'

'Don't be so hard on the boy, Alfred, he's only working his tip,' said a rather overweight, short man taking a 2-wood from his own caddy, who decided to stay silent after watching him strike the golf ball after Birchwood's, only for it to end up in the rough to the left of the green.

'Oh, bad luck, Martin, looks like you'll be getting the drinks in again,' Birchwood said, immediately cheered up by Martin's off shot.

'I bet you've been busy down there at GCHQ, what with that dreadful bombing and all these cyber attacks,' Birchwood said, a hint of sarcasm in his voice.

'Now, now, Alfred. You don't need to give me the I-told-you-so speech. You know I tried to get Project Spearhead approved, it's not my fault Giles Wright stonewalled you for his old university buddy's Ironclad system,' Martin said as the two of them walked leisurely down the fairway, the two caddies following a few metres back counting the minutes until the two ahead of them finished the round.

'Mmm, one would think the Minister for Security would have more say over the matter.'

'Don't be like that, old boy. Blame the PM, not me. He's the one who put Wright in charge of the NCSC.'

'Yes, but he's not the one bailing you out of your bad business decisions, is he, Martin?' said Birchwood, stopping to stare Martin Webster angrily in the eye. Martin shrivelled under Birchwood's gaze, relieved when he continued. 'Ironclad is more like a leaky sieve than a state-of-the-art cyber security system. What are they going to do now that Colin Trowbridge is dead?' Birchwood said, stopping by the edge of the green.

'That's as maybe, but Wright isn't about to let it go. It was his recommendation to spend the three hundred and fifty million pounds on Ironclad to protect the Ministry of Defence, the government, and the country's core amenity systems. He's not going to admit it's a bag of shit, is he? I told you the PM's got him flying back from holiday early for an emergency meeting at Nova South on Monday. Well, I found out this morning that Scott Miller has been invited to the meeting. Apparently, they're going to ask him if he'll take over and improve the Ironclad system.'

'What? When did this happen?'

'Last thing Friday I believe. Mr Miller has been assisting MI6 with the Genesis UK attacks and was recommended by Simon from Department D. The PM's given the proposal his full approval,' Martin said, heading for the rough to find his ball.

'Department what? Simon? Simon who?' Birchwood said, trying to keep his anger under control.

'Just Simon, it's a code name. Department D's top level, state security stuff, the King and the Prime Minister's eyes only. It was set up back in Churchill's days. *Wayhay*, I might not be buying the drinks after all,' Martin cheered, chipping his ball out of the rough and on to the green, where it rolled ever so slowly into the hole.

Birchwood turned to his caddie, fuming. 'Putter,' he said gruffly, grabbing it before walking over to his ball. His mind was racing. Even if his contract killer dealt with Giles Wright on Monday, with the PM, the security services, and this Simon character approving Scott Miller to take over Ironclad, his plans to finally get Project Spearhead pushed through the parliamentary committee to replace Ironclad would be dead in the water. No one would be singing his praises when he stopped the Genesis UK attacks, and gone would be the three hundred million price tag to implement Project Spearhead, plus the ten million pounds a year to run it. He took the shot, cursing under his breath as the ball rolled to a halt a few centimetres short of the hole. Out of the corner of his eye, he caught his caddy sniggering, but said nothing. No longer in the mood for golf, Birchwood took his phone out of his pocket and put on a concerned face while pretending to read a message.

'Sorry, Martin, something's come up. I'm going to have to leave,' Birchwood said, sliding the mobile back into his pocket and handing his putter to the caddy.

'Really? Nothing too serious, I hope,' Martin said in surprise.

'No, no, just something that requires my immediate attention,' Birchwood replied, heading towards the clubhouse with Martin and the two caddies following behind.

Martin took his clubs from the caddie and tipped him before placing the clubs in the boot of his car. Birchwood took the clubs from the caddie when they arrived at his Bentley, turning his back to him as he put them into the boot. When he shut the boot and turned, the young man was still standing there.

'Fuck off,' he spat, walking past the young man to head towards the clubhouse.

'Arsehole,' the caddie muttered under his breath, heading off to join Martin's caddie standing by the golf hire shop.

'I take it you didn't get a tip off that old bastard,' he said, seeing his friend's face as he walked over.

'Nah, tight-arsed prick, how about you?'

'Yep,' he replied, crinkling a twenty-pound note between his fingers.

They stood and watched as Birchwood came out of the clubhouse and got into his car.

'Tom!' came a shout from the clubhouse, making them turn their heads to see the manager waving him over.

'Yes sir, coming,' Tom said, heading over.

'Tom, we've had some serious complaints. I'm afraid we're going to have to let you go. Clean out your locker and hand in your pass,' the manager said as Tom's face fell.

In the background Birchwood drove by on his way out, his mouth curling up into a smile as he put his foot down and drove away, the feeling of satisfaction slipping away as his mind returned to the newly presented problem of Scott Miller.

'Call Nick Temple,' Birchwood said out loud.

'Calling Nick Temple, Head of Security at Birchwood Technologies,' came the car's slightly robotic female voice, while the contact details and connecting message displayed on the LCD screen in the centre of the dashboard.

'Mr Birchwood,' came Nick Temple's monotone, businesslike response through the car's speakers.

'Nick, I have a job for you and your associates. Off the books.'

'Ok, go ahead,' Temple answered, his voice still flat and businesslike.

'Not on the phone. I'll meet you at Birchwood Technologies in twenty minutes.'

The line cut dead without a reply from Temple. Birchwood wasn't surprised, Temple was blunt and to the point and, more importantly, always got the job done.

CHAPTER 18

Johnson drove out of a secured parking depot on the outskirts of London. He pulled into the nearest petrol station and put just enough fuel in to fulfill his needs. After paying with cash, he drove the white VW van he'd bought with cash when he arrived in the UK out of the petrol station and joined the M1 heading north, before taking the M25 eastbound and driving all the way around to the Thurrock turnoff. Ten minutes later he was in Tilbury, driving along Dock Road. A tired mix of small scrap yards, tyre garages and scruffy work units lined the right-hand side of the road, with glimpses of cranes, cargo ships and cruise ships moored in Tilbury Docks behind them. Council housing and flats lined the left-hand side of the road, with small and old cars parked outside that reflected the poverty in the area.

Spotting his destination on the right, Johnson drove straight past a small lock-up unit tucked behind a concrete block wall, its blocks barely visible under unkempt bushes and weeds growing up its side. He took in the open metal and wire gate in his peripheral vision until it was out of sight, and turned his attention to the council house windows and cars lining the road ahead as he drove on. Nobody was about, no people sitting in cars, no shadows or twitching curtains in the houses, no agents looking out of place dressed as utility workers in clean, newly signed vans that had never seen a day's work. A little way down the road, he turned around and drove back, turning through the open metal and wire gate into the small courtyard. He manoeuvred the van around and parked next to a blue Nissan Micro by the metal shuttered loading door. Johnson got out and stood next to the van, looking in every direction, listening for anything out of place. When nothing presented itself, he walked over and knocked on the rusty but solid looking door to one side of the loading bay. A small square hatch slid to one side and a pair of eyes stared suspiciously back at him.

'Robson?'

'Who the fuck wants to know?' he growled back.

'Montana. I've come to pick up a special order,' Johnson said.

'You got the money?' the man on the inside replied, his tone softening with the anticipation of getting paid.

Johnson pulled a fat brown envelope from the inside pocket of his jacket, flipping it open he thumbed across the wedge of fifty pound notes. Robson slammed the hatch shut. A heavy metallic screech and thumping sound followed from the other side of the door as he took a metal reinforcing bar out of its hooks and unlocked it. When it opened, a scruffy, nervous-looking man stuck his head out and looked around behind Johnson, checking that everything was clear before beckoning him in. As soon as he was inside, Robson shut the door and locked it behind them. When he turned back, his body language changed, he relaxed and smiled.

'So you're the Yank. I thought you'd be bigger. You want a drink? Tea, coffee?' he said, shuffling past him to a once white, now dirty grey, fingerprint-covered kettle.

'No, I'm good. You got everything I asked for?' Johnson said, looking around at the junk-filled shelves, wondering if he'd been misled about this fixer's abilities to supply almost anything someone in his business would need.

'Oh, ok, straight to business it is then,' said Robson, putting the kettle back down to walk to the back of the unit where he whipped a tarpaulin off a large flight case.

He wheeled it over to Johnson, kicked the brake down on the casters before twisting the metal locks around and lifting the lid. Johnson reached in and picked up a Heckler and Koch G36 assault rifle, checking the chamber before releasing the magazine.

'It's all there, rifle, standard issue handgun. The spare mags are in a box at the bottom along with the plastic, detonators and timers you asked for.'

Johnson put the rifle down and checked the handgun, helmet and items of clothing.

'You want a bag for that lot? No charge,' Robson said with a grin, pulling a large canvas bag from one of the shelving racks.

'This is all current, yeah?' Johnson said, looking Robson in the eye as he handed him the bag.

'Current, hell yeah, it's all brand new. I've got a man on the inside. This lot came direct from their own supply stores.'

'Good.'

'It's been a pleasure doing business with you. Now I just need the money and you can be on your way,' Robson said, trying not to sound nervous as Johnson looked at him while sliding a magazine into the handgun.

'I'll try the uniform on first,' said Johnson, placing the gun down on the flight case, much to Robson's relief.

He took his jacket off and pulled his sweatshirt up and over his head. It lifted his T-shirt up as he pulled it off, exposing the dressings on the rope burns and a tattoo of a skeleton frog holding a trident with the words "The only easy day was yesterday" tattooed below it.

'Nice tat,' Robson said, admiring it.

Johnson didn't reply. He quickly pulled his T-shirt down before trying the grey overall and tactical gear on. It fitted perfectly, so he changed back out of it, folded it neatly before putting it in the canvas bag along with the weapons, explosives and other bits in the flight case. Johnson zipped it up and took the envelope out of his jacket pocket, handing to Robson, who took it greedily. He flicked through the notes counted them as Johnson hefted the heavy bag onto his shoulder, making ready to leave.

'You need anything else, you give me a call, ok?'

'I won't, and you never saw me, you understand?' Johnson said, his eyes locked onto Robson's with a cold unblinking stare.

'Yeah sure, Montana who?' Robson said with a nervous laugh.

Robson moved to the door and slid the hatch open. He looked out to make sure the coast was clear. Satisfied all was quiet, he closed the hatch and lifted the locking bar off its hooks to open the door. Johnson stepped out into the sunshine and paced towards the van. The door to Robson's unit slammed shut behind him, the screeching sound of the bar being placed back into position following it. After putting the bag into the back of the van, Johnson climbed into the driver's seat and started the engine. He looked at his watch before driving across the yard to exit onto the road.

Ten past eleven, I'd better get a move on. There's a lot to set up before the meeting on Monday.

Focusing on his surroundings, Johnson spent a minute scanning the road and all vehicles in both directions for anything suspicious. When nothing presented itself, he pulled out and headed back towards London, taking care to use a different route than the one he used to get there. Being predictable led to being caught, and the man who chased him at the Red Lion and again at the apartment had gotten closer to him than anyone had before.

CHAPTER 19

'How's the head this morning?'

'It's ok, the lump's gone down. My neck still hurts a bit when I move it,' Danny said, grimacing as he pulled his T-shirt over his head and tried to look sideways across the bed at Nikki cleaning her teeth in the ensuite bathroom.

'Good, it might remind you to stop putting yourself in positions where you get blown up or shot at,' she said, taking the toothbrush out of her mouth and pointing it at him with a frown on her face to drive her words home.

'Jeez, the honeymoon period didn't last long, did it?' Danny said, giving her a big grin.

There was a second of silent tension before her face softened and she smiled back.

'I don't want you getting hurt, that's all, you could have been killed,' she said, walking over to him to give him a kiss, leaving him with a minty fresh taste on his lips.

'It was just bad luck, that's all, wrong place, wrong time. Ok. Look at me, I'm young, fit and healthy.'

'Have you looked in the mirror lately? You're not that young anymore,' she said, returning to brushing her teeth.

Danny looked over into the mirrored wardrobe door. The lines etched into his face from all the things he'd seen and done looked back at him. More things than any one man should have. She was right. He wasn't that young anymore.

'When is Scott picking you up?' Nikki called from the bathroom, her question creating a welcome distraction from his thoughts.

'Er, in about forty minutes,' Danny replied, looking at his old G-Shock watch.

'I'll be gone by then. Tell his royal highness I've gone to see the Anderson client about a new server system.'

'Will do. How is working for your brother going?'

'Not too bad. I'm getting used to it. I only want to kill him about half the time now instead of all the time. How do I look?' Nikki laughed, pulling on a navy blue suit jacket over her blouse.

'Like the best thing that ever happened to me,' Danny said in a melancholy way.

'Hey, what's got into you? Here, give us a kiss. I've got to go,' she said, kissing him before heading out the door and down the stairs, shouting, 'I'll see you tonight,' behind her.

Danny watched her out of the bedroom window, then went downstairs and made himself a coffee while he waited for Scott. The time Scott said he was going to pick him up came and went. Danny called him but it just went to answer phone. He waited another fifteen minutes then called Scott's apartment, only to get another answer phone message. When he was over an hour late, Danny'd had enough. He grabbed his car keys then rummaged through the drawer in the sideboard until he found Scott's spare set of keys and entry fob given to him in case of an emergency. Grabbing his jacket, Danny headed out the door, firing up his BMW M4 before heading towards central London and Scott's Greenwich apartment situated on the banks of the River Thames with views of the Isle of Dogs and the city's centre. He called Scott several times en route only to get the answer phone each time.

'Scott, where the hell are you, mate? Call me back,' Danny said, leaving another message. He was feeling a little apprehensive, but not that worried, not yet.

Scott ran a very successful business with clients all over the world. He could have quite easily had an emergency meeting or an IT problem that had to be dealt with. For some of his clients, an hour with systems down could cost millions. Touching the fob onto the post by the barrier for the underground parking, Danny drove down the ramp and parked his car in Scott's visitor parking bay, noticing that all four of Scott's cars were in their bays. Ignoring the lift as usual, Danny headed up the stairs, taking them two at a time. No matter how quiet it was, he never took the lift. Even though it was a long time since he was in the SAS, getting in a tin can that couldn't be defended and could easily be turned into a kill box still didn't sit well with him.

When he reached the top floor, he took out Scott's keys only to find the door to the apartment slightly ajar. His entire body language changed in the blink of an eye. Muscles tensed, his legs bent slightly as he rolled his feet from heel to toe, making no noise as he moved in close and put his ear to the crack to listen for any sounds of movement inside the apartment. In his hands, he manipulated the keys so the tips stuck out like makeshift knives between his fingers as he gripped the keyring end inside his fist.

The sound of the apartment door opening opposite him forced him into action. Danny twisted and moved the three paces across the hall in a second, his fist raised with two shiny keys pointing forwards, before the face of Scott's neighbour, Mr Chilvers, came into view. Mr Chilvers' face dropped and his eyes went wide in panic. He was about to yell out in surprise but stopped himself when Danny raised a finger to his lips and whispered, 'Back inside. Now.'

A very shocked Mr Chilvers did as he was told, shutting the door behind him as fast as he could. Danny returned to Scott's apartment door. Still no sound from within. He pushed the door gently open, slowing the speed down when the hinges started to creak. As soon as the gap was big enough, he slid inside and stood completely still, breathing steadily, slowing his heart rate so he could listen to the sounds of the apartment over its beating and the rushing of blood in his veins.

There were no telltale sounds of movement, no sixth sense of danger, just the usual sounds of the humming fridge freezer in the kitchen and the faint rumble of the central heating system. Moving out of the hall, Danny poked his head around the door to see into the open-plan kitchen, dining and lounge space. A cereal bowl lay broken on the floor, drying milk and muesli scattered across the tiles. The coffee table in the lounge sat to one side at a funny angle, and Scott's laptop bag and jacket were still sitting on the sofa with his car keys sitting on the arm. Moving on, Danny did a quick sweep of the bedrooms, then returned to the lounge before making a call.

'Danny,' Edward said bluntly.

'Ed, I need forensics and some agents over at Scott's. There are signs of a struggle and he's missing.'

'What? Ok, sit tight and don't touch anything. They'll be with you shortly,' Edward replied, hanging up straight afterwards.

Danny sat on one of the breakfast bar stools and looked around the apartment.

Where the fuck are you, Scotty boy?

CHAPTER 20

'This way, sir,' said one of Giles Wright's personal protection officers as he led the CEO of the National Cyber Security Centre out of Heathrow Airport arrivals hall.

They stopped just inside the exit doors while another protection officer went outside and checked it was clear to proceed to the escort cars parked just outside in a pick up bay.

'RT2 to RT1, all clear to proceed,' the protection officer codenamed RT2 said over his earpiece as he moved to the vehicle in front, opening the back door ready for Mr Wright.

'RT1, I'm bringing the principal out. This way, Mr Wright,' the protection officer just inside the exit doors said, sticking close to Mr Wright's side as they walked across to the car.

Wright got in first, before the officer closed the door. As he got into the front passenger seat, his fellow officer, RT2, moved to the escort vehicle behind them.

'RT1 to control, the principal is on the move.'

'Copy that, RT1,' came a voice over his earpiece as the two BMW X5's moved smoothly out of the pickup bay to start their journey to the Nova South building for Mr Wright's meeting.

'Is all this absolutely necessary?' Wright asked from the back.

'Sorry sir, there's a critical threat level in force. It's for your own safety, sir,' the officer said, twisting back in the front seat to give Wright a reassuring smile, his suit jacket opening just enough for the Glock 17 handgun tucked in its shoulder holster to show.

'Yes, of course. Sorry, it's been a long flight. Er, what's your name?'

'Thomas, sir, Thomas Trent.'

'Well, thank you, Thomas. I have some calls to make, so I'll leave you alone to do your job,' Wright said with a smile.

'Thank you, sir,' Thomas said, turning back around to face the front.

The journey took around fifty minutes, with the traffic moving slower as they approached central London. Giles Wright spent most of that time on his phone with various ministers and officials discussing the recent Genesis UK attacks.

'RT1 to control, arriving with the principal in approximately three minutes.'

'Control to RT1, counter terrorism officers are on site and have been notified of your arrival.'

'Affirmative, control.'

They pulled up by the gap left between the concrete barriers for arriving officials. An armed personal protection officer stepped forward to open the rear passenger door for Giles Wright while Thomas Trent got out of the front. He looked up and down the road before giving an acknowledging nod to the two counter terrorism officers standing either side of the entrance doors to Nova South. They nodded back, dressed in grey overalls with police identification patches on the arms and tactical vests visible behind the rifles they held across their chests, only their eyes showing from above their face masks and below their helmets.

As Giles Wright stepped through the gap in the concrete barriers, explosive devices buried in the planters down the pedestrian walkway running along the side of the Nova South building detonated. The blast took out the glass along the side of the building. Bits of concrete planter, soil, and glass crystals bounced and slid across the shiny marble floor of the foyer. To add to the shock and confusion, a third device planted in a bin outside a shop across the road exploded, causing cars to swerve and skid in panic. A counter terrorism officer came running through the cloud of smoke and dust from the walkway and headed towards them.

'Get him back in the car. Now,' he yelled, pushing Giles Wright back into the rear of the vehicle before jumping in behind him. 'Go, go, go, get him out of here,' he yelled as Thomas Trent jumped back into the front passenger seat.

The driver sped away just as Thomas pulled the car door shut, the escort vehicle accelerating to follow close behind.

'RT1 to control, we are evacuating the principal.'

'Control to RT1, proceed to the safe zone. Officers are on the way to rendezvous with you.'

'What the hell happened?' Thomas said, turning in his seat to look out the rear window at the smoke and panic and chaos at Nova South as it shrank into the distance.

He turned his attention to the counter terrorism officer to see his brown eyes over the mask staring straight back at him. Something was wrong. The look on Thomas's face giving away his suspicions as he reached for his gun. A series of pops sounded long before he got to it. The air left his lungs like he'd been hit in the chest with a sledgehammer. Thomas looked down to see a bloody stain washing down his crisp white shirt. He noticed the glove box in front of him hanging off, shattered by the bullets that went through the back of his chair and through him, before embedding themselves into the plastic. His world went black, and he slumped forward in his chair.

Johnson whipped the silenced Glock 17 up from behind the seat and pushed the end into Giles Wright's chest, pulling the trigger twice, killing him instantly. All this happened in a matter of seconds. By the time the driver realised what was happening, Johnson had leaned forward and placed the hot end of the silencer on the back of his neck.

'There's a road coming up on the left. Take it,' he growled, jabbing the end of the gun harder into the driver's flesh to leave no doubt who was in control of the situation.

CHAPTER 21

As soon as the forensics team arrived at Scott's apartment they told Danny to leave so they could seal it off and get on with their job. Frustrated and feeling like a spare part, Danny left them to it and headed back to the SIS building. After waiting for security to get Edward's authorisation so they could issue him a visitor's pass, Danny went through the rigmarole of clearing the scanner and metal detector before heading up to the operations room, hoping they might have a lead into Scott's disappearance. When he entered, the room was in chaos. People moved around, urgent discussions and questions flew across the room and phones rang continuously.

'What's going on?' he asked after finding Edward at the front of the room.

'There's been some explosions at the Nova South building.'

'Christ, how many casualties are there?'

'Thankfully none, personal protection officers got the NCSC's CEO, Giles Wright, away from the site as soon as it happened. They're still in transit. Luckily, the prime minister, along with various members of the security council, including

Simon, were safely tucked away in a third-floor meeting room.'

'An explosion in the building and there are no casualties?' Danny said, surprised.

'The explosion wasn't in the building. Two devices detonated in planters on the walkway to one side and a third device detonated in a bin across the street.'

'Doesn't that strike you as odd?' Danny said, frowning.

Edward was about to answer when radio chatter came over speakers at the front of the room.

'RT2 to control, I've lost radio contact with RT1. Can you identify the counter terrorism officer who got into the car with the principal?'

'Control to RT2, maintain escort to primary vehicle while we try to get comms back and check who the counter terrorism officer is.'

'Copy that, control.'

'The explosions were a decoy. Wright was the target. The counter terrorism officer is an imposter,' said Danny in a raised voice.

It took a second for Danny's words to sink in before Edward sprang into action.

'Patch me into control. Now!' he yelled.

'You're in sir,' came a voice seconds later.

'Control, this is Secret Intelligence Service Director Edward Jenkins. We believe the primary vehicle has been compromised. Instruct escort vehicle to intercept and detain suspect posing as counter terrorism officer.'

'This is control, received and understood,' came the response over the speaker before Edward's orders were forwarded to the escort vehicle. 'RT2, this is control. The primary vehicle has been compromised, intercept and protect the principal. The counter terrorism officer is a suspected hostile.'

'Who's the protection officer in the primary vehicle?' Danny said to Edward.

'Er, hang on,' Edward said, turning to address the room. 'Can someone tell me who RT1 is?'

'He's one of ours, sir. Thomas Trent. Simon requested him personally to escort Mr Wright.'

'Shit, it's Tom,' Danny said at the mention of his friend's name.

'Sir, we have the GPS location of the vehicles coming up on screen now,' said one of Edward's agents, distracting the two of them to look at two moving dots on a satellite map of London with the street names and places overlaid across the top.

'RT2 to control, we are moving in to intercept the primary vehicle.'

The tension in the room built as everyone watched the location dot for RT2's vehicle close the gap on the primary vehicle.

CHAPTER 22

Johnson swung his head to look at the escort vehicle closing in behind them as they flew down a narrow access road. He turned back to look out the front, his eyes locked on a white VW van parked a little way up ahead, with a traffic warden busily sticking a parking ticket onto its front windscreen. The warden looked up as Johnson flew past, his head swinging back at the escort vehicle giving chase. The traffic warden and personal protection officer's eyes met as the car drew level with the white VW van. At the same time, Johnson pressed the button on a small transmitter in his free hand. The van and traffic warden instantly disappeared inside the blast, an array of nuts, bolts and ball bearings shredding RT2's vehicle, killing everyone inside. The car continued on under its own momentum before hitting the corner of a building, bringing it to an abrupt stop.

'Take the next right,' Johnson ordered.

The driver did as he was told, his face white as a sheet as he looked at Johnson in the rear view mirror. They flew down a tree-lined back road with three-storey Georgian townhouses on either side, braking hard before a sharp turn to the right to cross over the Grand Union canal.

'Stop here.'

The driver did as he was told, his head fixed firmly ahead while he flicked his eyes to look at Johnson in the rear view mirror, sure that he was going to blow his brains out at any moment.

'Are you going to kill me?' he said, his mouth dry and voice shaky.

'Give me your wallet,' Johnson replied, ignoring the comment. He put his free hand between the front car seats and beckoned with his fingers for the wallet.

The driver moved to pull the wallet out of his trouser pocket.

'Slowly,' Johnson added, tapping the end of the suppressor on the back of the driver's head.

He handed the wallet over and Johnson flipped it open one-handed, resting it on the seat beside him so he could slide the driving license out to look at the name and address on it.

'You married, Terry, kids?'

'Yes, two kids, boys,' Terry answered.

'Nice. Here's what you're going to do. I'm going to get out and you're going to drive away, and keep driving until you're at least two miles away from here. You got that, Terry.'

The driver just nodded nervously.

'Good, because if you don't and I see anyone even so much as give me a sideways look, I know your name and where you live, and I will find you and your family. And when I do, I will kill them in front of you. Do you understand me, Terry?'

Terry looked at Johnson in the rear view mirror and nodded. Johnson opened the door and started to get out before turning back.

'Two miles, Terry and you don't contact anyone, ok?'

Terry turned his head and nodded. Johnson's eyes stared at him intensely over the top of his mask before getting out and shutting the door. He watched the car move off and didn't move until it was no longer in sight. Turning around, Johnson headed down the steps to one side of the bridge, taking the pathway along the side of the Grand Union canal, nodding to a couple of dog walkers who looked apprehensively at him in his counter terrorism officer uniform.

'Nothing to worry about, folks, just a routine check,' Johnson said, the comment seeming to satisfy the couple, although he didn't really care if they phoned it in as suspicious. By the time anyone worked out where he'd been dropped off, he'd be long gone. As soon as they were out of sight, Johnson stepped onto a brightly painted narrowboat and went inside. While he changed into the neatly folded pile of clothes on the small kitchen table, he checked the time on his watch.

A mile and a half away, Terry continued to drive without stopping or calling it in. He'd got his breathing under control and his pounding heart had finally dropped under a hundred beats a minute. Half a mile later, he pulled the car over and looked at Thomas Trent's body beside him. Releasing his seat belt so he could lean over, he pulled Trent's radio out of his pocket.

'Hello, this is Terry McCann, RT1 and the principal are down. I'm at—'

The explosive device Johnson had placed under the front seat while they were driving detonated, silencing Terry as it blew the windows out and folded the roof back like an open sardine tin.

Two miles away, Johnson emerged from the narrowboat in new clothes, a flat cap and sunglasses. He untied the moorings and started the engine before chugging gently off down the river, giving a friendly wave to fellow holidaymakers cruising past in the opposite direction.

CHAPTER 23

A deafening roar of distorted noise boomed out from the speakers in the MI6 control room. Agents listening on headphones yanked them off quickly, the sound from the exploding van hurting their ears. RT2's radio set went dead and the primary vehicle moved steadily away from the stationary flashing dot of RT2's vehicle.

'It's him, the guy from the Red Lion bombing. I know it's him,' Danny said through clenched teeth.

'Director Jenkins to control, what is your ETA for interception of primary vehicle?' Edward said anxiously.

'Control to Director Jenkins, an armed response vehicle is en route to intercept, ETA approximately three minutes.'

'They've stopped,' Danny said, staring at the dot on the map.

'Must be traffic, look they're moving again,' Edward said beside him.

The room fell into silence as the red dot continued for a little while, then stopped again.

'ARV212 to control, we are approaching Randolph Avenue, ETA to intercept the primary vehicle is thirty seconds.'

There was some crackly static on the comms before the driver of the primary vehicle's voice came out of the control centre's speakers.

'Hello, this is Terry McCann. RT1 and the principal are down. I'm at—'

For the second time in only a few minutes, a deafening roar of distorted noise boomed out from the speakers, sending the room into shocked silence.

'AVR212 to control, we have a visual on the primary vehicle. It's been destroyed by an explosive device and is on fire. The flames are too intense to see if anyone's inside and there is no sign of the occupants outside the vehicle. Requesting fire service to attend while we corner off the area.'

'Control to AVR212, receiving you loud and clear. Fire service and Metropolitan Police units are en route and will be with you soon.'

'Shit,' Danny yelled, thumping his fist down on a desk in frustration.

'Ok, listen up, until we know otherwise we do this by the book. Work on all scenarios, the kidnap of Giles Wright and Thomas Trent, the possibility of vehicle swaps, all CCTV in the area, and the identity of the counter terrorism officer. Get to work,' Edward said, addressing the silenced room, which exploded into a hive of activity the second he'd finished.

'There's no point. They're all dead, and he's long gone,' Danny said to Edward, his face hardening while his eyes turned dark and dangerous. He turned and barged his way through two of Edward's agents standing behind him as he headed for the door.

'You don't know that for sure,' Edward said, moving between his men to follow him.

'I do. I've looked into the man's eyes, and I've seen him move. He's a trained killer, a professional, he's no kidnapper.'

'That's as maybe, but we've got a description of what he

looks like and forensics from the apartment are being DNA screened. We'll soon find out his identity.'

'No, you won't. He's a ghost. You won't find him in the system. All I know is he's ex-military, probably special forces, hell, he might even be a US government asset,' Danny said, continuing to head for the exit.

'Again, you don't know that. Let's just wait until forensics get back to us. Danny, just hold up, where are you going?' Edward said, stepping in front of him just before he left the control room.

'Look, they're dead and he's gone, and Scott's still missing. I can't just stand around here doing nothing. First, I'm going to find Scott, and then I'm going to find the American and make him pay for killing Tom and John,' Danny said, only just about keeping a lid on the anger burning inside him.

'Danny, just calm down, will you? You're going to do nothing of the sort. We're doing everything we can to find Scott and the American, but we will do it with evidence and intelligence. I don't need vigilantes running around London causing chaos, ok? Just go home and cool off. I'll call you as soon as I know anything,' Edward said, ignoring his ringing phone to maintain eye contact with Danny while he spoke.

Danny stood his ground and held Edward's gaze for a long time until he eventually nodded and walked around Edward to leave the room.

'Jenkins,' Edward snapped down his phone as he turned back into the control room.

'Edward, it's Simon. I need a status report,' Simon said, with the alarms and sirens from the chaos around the Nova building wailing in the background.

Edward rubbed his forehead and sighed before running through everything he knew.

Five minutes later Danny got into his car. Reaching into his jacket pocket he pulled out the MI6 ID wallet he'd lifted from one of Edward's agents as he barged through them. He looked enough like the tiny photo to pass a quick flash if needed. Putting it back in his pocket, he drove his BMW M4 out of the SIS building's underground car park. When the barrier opened, Danny turned onto Albert Embankment and followed it along the banks of the River Thames, slowing for the roundabout by Lambeth Bridge. Danny frowned as he indicated left to go over the bridge and head through central London on his way home. He pulled to a stop, giving way to a car coming around the roundabout. When it passed he didn't move off. His head turned from his way home across Lambeth Bridge to straight on towards Scott's Greenwich apartment. The sound of impatient car horns beeping behind him forcing a decision.

'Fuck it,' he muttered. Turning the indicator off he drove straight over, heading towards Greenwich.

CHAPTER 24

Scott had been in the back of the Transit van for what seemed like an eternity. He sat on the floor with his hands cable tied behind his back, some sort of hessian material hood was over his head, which allowed him to see little pinpricks of light when the van turned north and the midday sun poured into the back of the van through the rear window. Scott tried to think what Danny would do and felt around for something sharp that he could rub the cable ties on to cut them. After a few minutes of rubbing his hands along the side, Scott found a sharp screw head poking out of the wood paneling that covered the interior in the back of the van. He had to shuffle up into a crouch to get his wrists high enough to rub the plastic zip ties onto the burred end of the screw. Trying to stay balanced as the van moved around, Scott rubbed the plastic tie up and down as fast as he could, trying to cut through it.

'Oi, pack it in,' came a shout from the front, followed up a second later by a hand gripping him by the scruff of his neck and yanking him to the floor. 'Sit bloody still. You try anything like that again and I'm going to start breaking bones. You understand me?' the man in the front growled before turning back to sit down in the front passenger seat.

Scott reluctantly did as he was told. Sliding back to sit against the side of the van, he could feel the warmth of the sun through the rear window and turned his head to see the tiny pinpricks of bright light through the hessian weave.

Right, think, Scott. It's around midday and the sun should be due south. It's behind us, so we must be moving north. We are still moving steadily, so we must be on a main road, possibly the A12. It's not been too long. Could be Stratford, or maybe further out, maybe Wanstead. Good Lord, if I broke out here I'd probably be safer inside the van.

Despite not knowing what he'd do with that knowledge, Scott's assumptions were surprisingly accurate. The van passed through Wanstead on the A12 to join the A406, which led them onto the M11 motorway heading out of London towards Cambridge. They drove for around twenty minutes before pulling off into Birchanger Services near Stansted Airport, following the slip road around into the car park before parking up in the far corner.

'Change the plates,' came a voice from the front, followed by the two front doors opening.

When the doors slammed shut, Scott sensed he was alone in the van. Seizing the moment, Scott turned and slid his face around on the panelling until the screw head caught on the hessian material. Jerking back, he pulled until the material ripped and pinged off the screw, the sudden release making him lose balance and fall onto his back. Rolling up onto his knees, Scott swung his head from left to right, until one blue eye looked out through the tiny hole in the material. Seeing the door release handle on the inside of the sliding door, Scott stood up as straight as he could in the confined space and turned his back to the door. Feeling around until he found the handle, he pulled it up. As the door popped open and slid to one side, Scott disappeared as he fell backwards through the gap, landing heavily in the parking space next to the van. He swung his sack-covered head from left to right, looking through the hole to see a pair of legs facing him at the front of the van and another pair of legs at the rear. With fear and adrenaline kicking in, Scott rolled up onto his feet and started running between the parked cars, shaking his sack covered head every time the material flopped forward to cover the view of where he was going through the hole.

'Help, help!' he yelled at the top of his voice.

'Fuck, get him, quickly, before people see him,' came a shout from behind him.

Scott got a brief view of the entrance to the services on the far side of the car park and turned to run between the cars in its direction. As footsteps got louder behind him, the cloth sack moved again and he lost sight of where he was going. Still running at full pelt, Scott slammed into the front of a parked car. Pain shot through his shins and knees as the top half of his body folded forward and he smacked head first into the bonnet. Winded and in pain, Scott tried to suck in a breath and get up. Hands grabbed him before he could set off again, and dragged him off the bonnet. As they pulled him upright, he got a glimpse of a man standing up ahead with a nervous I don't want to get involved look on his face. As they pulled Scott away, his view got blocked by the back of one of his captures heads as they stepping in front of him.

'It's alright, mate. Reluctant stag, he'll be alright after a few beers and a stripper,' he said, laughing.

The man relaxed a little and managed a nervous laugh in return. Back at the van, they bundled Scott into the back, one man climbing in behind him while the other slid the side door shut and jumped into the driver's seat.

'Fucking shut up and lie still,' growled the man in the back before punching Scott hard in the side. 'Pass me some more ties,' he said, turning to the driver.

While still trying to get his breath, Scott felt his ankles

being zip tied together before being yanked up behind him and zip tied to his wrists, leaving him hogtied uncomfortably on the floor of the van. Reaching down, the man grabbed the sack on Scott's head and twisted it around so the hole was at the back and he could no longer see.

'Let's get the fuck out of here before someone calls the police,' said the third man, as he got into the passenger seat.

The van started and with Scott pinned to the floor by the man in the back, they swiftly pulled out of the services and turned back onto the motorway, continuing their journey towards Cambridge.

CHAPTER 25

The white forensics van and MI6 vehicles had left Scott's apartment building by the time Danny arrived. Just a single police patrol car remained outside the entrance door. He used Scott's key fob to open the barrier and drove down into the underground car park. He parked in the same space as earlier and continued with a déjà vu feeling from earlier that morning as he headed up the stairs to Scott's penthouse apartment.

'Anyone still here?' said Danny confidently, showing his stolen ID to the bored police constable under orders to contain the crime scene.

'No, the last one left about an hour ago.'

'So what are you still doing here?' Danny asked, pushing the apartment door open.

'We haven't got any keys to lock up, so I've got to wait for the locksmith to secure the apartment,' the officer replied grumpily.

'Put a call in to cancel him on your way out. I'll lock up when I've finished,' Danny said, pulling Scott's keys out of his pocket and rattling them in front of the officer.

'Oh, right, very good, sir,' the officer said, perking up at being discharged from his task as he walked over to the lift and stabbed the call button.

Danny went inside, closing the door behind him. He moved slowly into the lounge, taking in every detail, but not really knowing what exactly he was looking for. After doing a circuit of the apartment, he moved over to the bi-folding glass doors, glancing at a picture of him, Scott and Nikki on his way. Pushing the growing anger and frustration at Scott's disappearance and the murder of his friends Thomas Trent and John Ball down deep, Danny looked out across the terrace at the Thames and glass and steel skyscrapers of central London in the distance. He sighed as he panned away from the Thames to look at a tired, ten-storey block of housing association flats sitting opposite Scott's multi-million pound apartment building.

As his eyes floated over the windows, an old man sitting in his comfy chair looking in his direction out of his lounge window caught his eye. Neither of them moved. Danny thought perhaps the old man was just absentmindedly looking out the window and couldn't see him through the reflection in the glass doors. The notion was proven wrong when he raised his arm and gave a wave to the old man. With no change of expression the old man lifted his arm slowly and gave a wave back. As he lowered it, a middle-aged woman in a nurse's or carer's uniform came into view. She said some-thing to the old man then looked in Danny's direction. Danny waved then pointed to his mouth before pointing at them. The woman looked confused for a second until she got that he wanted to talk to them, then nodded back at him. Danny gave her a thumbs up, counting the floors to the old man's flat before heading out of Scott's apartment and down the stairs. He crossed the small park between the two buildings and found the entrance door to the flats. Counting the buzzers, Danny pressed the one for the old man's flat and waited.

'Hello,' came a woman's voice.

'Hi, I'm a government agent looking into the disappearance of a Mr Miller in the penthouse apartment opposite. I wondered if I could have a word with the gentleman sitting in the window.'

'Reg, hang on, I'll just go and ask him,' she replied, the door intercom going quiet.

Danny looked at his watch impatiently while he waited.

'Ok, come on up,' crackled over the intercom before the door lock buzzed open.

Danny pushed his way in and headed up the stairs to the seventh floor flat. The door opened as he approached and the woman stood in the opening to greet him.

'Hi, I'm Sandy, Reggie's home help. Do you mind if I see some ID? You know, you can't be too careful,' she said with a smile.

'Yes, sorry, of course,' Danny replied, flashing the stolen ID just long enough for the MI6 agent part to be read.

'Ok, come in. Reggie is through here. I'm not sure how much help he will be. He can be a little vague these days,' she said, leading Danny into the lounge. 'Reggie, love, the man from across the road is here to ask you a few questions.'

'Huh, man? What man?' Reggie said without turning away from the window.

'Hello Reggie, we just waved to each other. I was in the penthouse apartment across the way,' Danny said in a calm and friendly voice.

Reggie looked away from the window, his eyes fixing on Danny as his forehead wrinkled into a frown.

'You're not him, you're not the party boy from over there, the one with the flash cars and a different woman friend every other night.'

He knows Scott then.

'No, he's my friend. He went missing this morning. I wondered if you saw anything?' Danny said, smiling at Reggie even though the old man was still frowning at him.

After an awkward pause and no response from Reggie, Danny looked at Sandy standing behind Reggie.

'Sorry, love, he has good days and bad,' she said with a shrug.

Danny turned back to Reggie to have a final go at getting through to him.

'Reggie, the party boy in the penthouse apartment over there, did you see him this morning? Was anyone with him?'

'Hello, I know you. You were over there. You waved at me,' Reggie said, turning back to the window to look at Scott's apartment.

'Yes, Reggie, that was me. It was nice to meet you,' Danny said, getting up to leave as he was getting nowhere.

'They put him in a van, the party boy. They put him in one of them Transit vans. A Vauxhall. No, no, that's not right, a Ford. It was a grey Ford Transit van, right there by the entrance, three men dressed in black with wolly mask things on their heads. They drove off in such a hurry they knocked one of them delivery boys over on their way out. You know, the mopeds with a blue food box on the back, what are they called, Kangaroo or something?'

Danny turned back in surprise. 'Deliveroo?'

'Yes, that's it, Deliveroo. The lad was fuming. He ran after them waving his phone in front of him.'

'What, his phone? Was he filming them or taking pictures?'

Reggie's eyes dulled and he drifted back to looking out the window without answering Danny's question.

'Thank you, Reggie, that's great. I'll be off now, but you take care of yourself.'

'Sorry, he drifts in and out,' Sandy said when Reggie didn't answer. He was looking out the window, lost in his thoughts.

Danny thanked her and left the flat, heading back to his car before reluctantly driving towards home.

CHAPTER 26

Danny pulled up outside his house. He opened the front door and went inside.

'Nikki, you home?' he shouted. No answer.

Heading upstairs, Danny entered the bedroom and went over to the wardrobe. He took the shoes and boxes out of the base and put them to one side, before pulling the false bottom to the wardrobe up, revealing two black holdalls sitting snugly in a box section built into the floor. He unzipped a holdall and did a quick check of the passports placed on top of bundles of cash. Peeling a wad of notes out, Danny put them in his jacket pocket and zipped the holdall back up. He lifted the other bag out and placed it on the bed and unzipped it. Reaching in, Danny took two Glock 17 handguns out and placed them on the bed before pulling out a stubby AR-15 semiautomatic rifle with a folding stock and silencer.

He clicked the stock into place and checked the firing mechanism before folding it back up and placing it back on the bed. Danny checked a Glock and spare magazines before laying it on the bed next to the rifle. He was checking the second Glock when a voice came from the bedroom door.

'Well, this doesn't look good,' came a voice from behind him.

Danny twisted his arm out and locked it in a fraction of a second, the barrel of the Glock pointing between the eyes of the person who spoke. He lowered the gun like lightning when he saw his wife standing in the doorway.

'Fuck. Sorry, you scared the shit out of me,' Danny said, walking over to Nikki to give her a hug.

'Says the man pointing a gun in my face,' Nikki said, giving him a hug before pulling away. 'Come on, spit it out. What's going on?'

Danny tucked the gun in the back of his jeans and sat on the bed.

'It's Scott. He didn't turn up this morning. When I went to his apartment he was gone and there were signs of a struggle. While I was trying to find out what happened to him, the CEO of the National Cyber Security Centre was abducted as he arrived at the Nova South building for a meeting, the same meeting Scott was supposed to be attending. It's the American, I know it. The one that blew up the Red Lion pub, the same one that killed John Ball the other day. He killed Wright and his driver and Thomas Trent. You remember Tom from the wedding? He was on duty as Wright's personal protection officer,' Danny said, sadness for his friends and concern for Scott written all over his face.

'Oh god, that's awful. What about Scott? You don't think he's dead do you?' Nikki said, putting her hand to her mouth as she sat down on the bed next to Danny in shock.

'No, no, he was taken. Three men put him in a van and drove off. If they wanted him dead, they would have killed him in his apartment,' Danny replied, putting his arm around her.

'Do you know who has taken him?' Nikki managed to say as tears filled her eyes.

'Not yet, but I'm working on it,' Danny said, holding her tight.

'That's why you're getting your gun?' replied Nikki after a minute.

Danny nodded, his face turning from concern to hard determination. It was a look Nikki knew well.

'What about Simon, MI6, Edward, the police?'

'They're spread thin with all these Genesis UK attacks and Scott's not a priority. I'll have to find him myself before the trail goes cold, or he outgrows his usefulness,' Danny said, his cheeks flexing as he clenched his teeth angrily.

Nikki stood up and moved around to stand in front of him. Cradling his head in her arms, she bent down as he looked up at her and kissed him. When they separated, she looked him in the eyes.

'Find my brother and bring him home,' she said, her tone deadly serious.

'I will, I promise,' Danny said, slowly standing up. 'I've got to go out for a bit. Don't worry, I won't be too long,' he added, picking the black holdall up and putting it neatly back under the floor in the wardrobe while leaving the other Glock tucked in the back of his jeans.

'Where are you going?' Nikki said, the kept gun not going unnoticed.

'I need to see where Tom died.'

'Ok. Take as long as you need. And Danny?'

'What?' Danny said, turning back to look at her.

'Be careful.'

'I always am,' he replied with a smile that did nothing to hide his sadness as he turned away and headed down the stairs.

He climbed into the driver's seat and started the engine. Glancing back at the house, Danny saw Nikki looking at him from the bedroom window. She gave him a single wave, which he returned before driving away.

CHAPTER 27

"Pressure on the Prime Minister for action is building today after the assassination of the CEO of the National Cyber Security Centre, Giles Wright. Mr Wright was taken after a series of explosions at the Nova South building in Victoria. A man posing as a counter terrorism officer gained access to Mr Wright's car while the security services evacuated Mr Wright from the scene. The car and its escort vehicle were later involved in a series of planned explosions killing all involved. The terrorist group Genesis UK has claimed responsibility through a flood of social media posts."

Danny reached forward and turned off the car radio as he got close to the area. A police car blocked the narrow access road where RT2's car had been destroyed. A police officer standing in front of it waved him on when he slowed to look. He could see the burnt wreckage of the van and escort vehicle fifty metres beyond the police car and streams of incident tape. Danny navigated his way through the back streets until he came out on the other side of the police cordon. Continuing along the route taken by Giles Wright's car, Danny glanced over at the longboats as the road bent sharply to the right and crossed over the Grand Union canal. He drove on until he came to a second police cordon and the grim sight of the burnt out lead vehicle. Danny got out and flashed his ID to the police officer as he ducked under the police tape, thankfully he didn't look at it too closely and didn't want to question an MI6 agent's authority for fear of getting bollocked by the sergeant back at the station. A coroner's van had removed what remained of the bodies earlier, leaving only the burnt-out husk of the car, destroyed to the point of being no help to forensics, which is precisely how the American planned it. Lines creased on Danny's forehand as a frown formed. He looked back up the road in the direction he came from.

The car stopped briefly while it was being tracked.

Ducking back under the tape, Danny got back in his car and did a three-point turn, heading back the way he came. He parked up just short of the bridge over the Grand Union canal and got out. Casting his mind back to the screen tracking the cars in the operations room, he realised the car had stopped exactly where he was parked.

It wasn't traffic. The bastard got out. Somehow, he made the driver continue driving while he got away.

Walking over to the bridge, Danny ran through scenarios in his head.

Was someone waiting to drive him away? No, this guy works alone. Did he have another vehicle parked as a getaway? No, that would be too risky with the chance of road blocks and his photofit picture being circulated he wouldn't want to risk it, and there are no train or underground stations around here.

Danny's eyes fell onto the steps down to the path beside the canal. He walked down and stood on the path, looking at the brightly painted narrowboats moored along the bank. One of them emerged from under the bridge, chugging its way along the canal with its owner steering from the back. He smiled and nodded as he passed, just a man on his boat, where he should be, forgettable, invisible.

The bastard just floated on out of here.

Seeing a moored-up narrowboat twenty metres away with smoke drifting up out of the steel chimney poking through the roof, Danny walked towards it. The narrow twin doors at the rear were open, and he could hear noises from within.

'Hello, anyone in?' he called from the canal path.

'Er, hello, yeah,' came a man's voice from within, swiftly followed by the head of a white guy with grungy-looking dreadlocks. The opt-out-of-society look continued when an arm full of bangles appeared, followed by the sight of his jumper that looked like it had been made out of the arse end of a camel.

'Hi, I'm agent Harris,' Danny said, having to look at the name on the stolen MI6 ID before flashing it at the guy. 'I'm just investigating the events from this morning. Do you live here on the boat, Mr…?'

'Mr Finnley, just call me Luke. Yeah, I live here,' Luke said with a big, friendly smile, showing lots of yellow teeth.

'Were you on the boat this morning, around 9:30 to 10:30?' Danny said, keeping the conversation light and friendly in return.

'Yeah, I was. I heard the van down the road when it exploded, came out but couldn't see anything from here, so I went back in.'

'Ok, did you see anyone come down the canal path, a counter terrorism officer - he would have been in full kit, helmet, mask, guns and body armour - or anyone looking out of place or suspicious?'

'Er, no. Sorry, man, I was down below. I was in the middle of cooking some vegan sausages when the van exploded, nearly burnt the buggers. Sorry I can't help.'

'Well, thanks anyway,' Danny said, turning to walk away.

'I did notice something strange, though,' Luke said, stopping Danny in his tracks.

'Yes?'

'Yeah, an old couple, Philip and Audrey. They moor their boat just there by the bridge. They don't go out in it as much as they used to. I think they've been advertising to sell it. Anyway, when I finished my sausages and cleared up, I came out and it was gone. I thought it was a little strange, because they usually come and have a chat with me when they're here.'

Danny turned and looked at the space where the boat had been, then turned back.

'What's the name of the boat?' he asked, the light and friendly changing to firm and serious.

'Moonbeams, it's a narrowboat like this.'

'Colour?'

'Navy blue with gold patterning around the windows.'

'Thanks. The couple, Philip and Audrey, do you know their last name?'

'Er, yeah it's Tennent. I think they live in Wimbledon somewhere.'

'Great. Thanks, Luke,' Danny said, heading back along the canal path and up the steps by the bridge, heading back towards his car.

As he reached the top step, he noticed a large black Audi Q7 parked behind his car. The driver's door opened and a figure he recognised as Simon's driver stepped out and walked around to the kerbside to open the rear passenger door. Danny walked over and looked inside at Simon, immaculately suited as always.

'Do get in without a fuss, Daniel, I've had enough dramatics for one day,' Simon said, his voice calm and in control as always.

Danny slid into the seat beside him without saying a word. The driver shut the door as soon as he was in and walked a few paces away from the car to give them privacy.

'Just out for a little stroll by the canal, are we?' Simon said arrogantly.

'It's a popular place. After all, you're here,' Danny replied defiantly.

'Indeed I am, Daniel, indeed I am. Well, let's cut to the chase, shall we? Now that our mutual friend David Tremain has retired, our new Minister for Security, Martin Webster, has been promising everyone he will bring Genesis UK to justice. Unfortunately, he's shutting my department out in favour of Special Branch, who quite frankly couldn't find Genesis UK if they were working out of their own basement, which is a distinct possibility. Anyway, myself and certain members of the security services think that in the interest of the state we should extricate matters and nip this in the bud before it spirals out of control.'

'Just tell me what you want, Simon,' Danny said, not interested in Simon's political explanations.

'I want you to do what you do best, Daniel, we both have mutual interests in putting this to bed. I need someone off the books who can find out who the American and Genesis UK are, and as far as I can tell you wish to get Mr Miller back and find the man who killed Thomas and John. We both know Scott's disappearance is too much of a coincidence not to be linked to Genesis UK. If you help me find Genesis UK, I promise you, once we find out who our American friend is, I will give you the opportunity to deal with him for Thomas and John.'

Danny sat in the back of the car in silence for what seemed like ages, his facial features dark and dangerous as he contemplated his answer.

'The American used a navy blue narrowboat called Moonbeams to get out of the area. It's owned by a Philip and Audrey Tennent.'

'He'll be long gone by now. I'll pass that little piece of information on to our Minister for Security. It'll give him something to shout about while we find out who Genesis UK are. Anything else?'

'The American had uniforms, guns and explosives. The meeting at Nova was arranged at short notice and he didn't bring them into the country with him. Someone had to supply them to him, someone good, well connected. There can't be too many fixers that could put their hands on a counter terrorism police uniform with standard issue rifle at such short notice.'

'One would think not. Good, is that it?'

'No, Scott was taken away in a grey Ford Transit van. I don't have a reg, but it knocked a Deliveroo rider off his bike as they left. The resident in the flat opposite thinks the rider was pointing his phone at it as it drove off. Find the Deliveroo guy and see if he took a picture of the van. I need to know where it went.'

'Consider it done,' Simon said, glancing at his watch to signify the meeting was over.

Danny opened the door, but looked back at Simon before stepping out.

'And if anyone from Genesis UK gets in my way?'

'Then perhaps the gun you have tucked in the back of your jeans might come in useful. If you can break a habit of a lifetime and keep it discreet, I will take care of it. If you destroy public property or accidentally kill any civilians, then you're on your own, dear boy.'

'Understood,' Danny replied, giving Simon a single nod before climbing out of the car.

'Daniel,' Simon called after him.

'What?' Danny said, annoyed, bending down to look back in the car.

'Thomas and John were good men, loyal men. Their deaths deserve to be avenged.'

Danny let the words sink in before standing upright and shutting the car door. He watched the driver get in and drive away before walking to his own car and heading home as the sun set in the sky.

CHAPTER 28

Johnson moored the narrowboat and made his way from the canal to a nearby busy high street. He wore a latex mask disguise that pulled on over his head and covered the top of his shoulders, the latex seam staying hidden from view under his buttoned-up shirt. The mask came complete with real human hair, made up into a full head of grey hair and a grey beard. Johnson fixed the holes around the eyes and mouth to the skin with prosthetic glue. With a pair of little round glasses and a baseball cap, it gave him the realistic appearance of a man in his fifties. He hailed a cab and headed to St Pancras station, paying with cash at the other end. Putting his rucksack on his back, Johnson wheeled a medium-sized suitcase into the station. He headed away from the platforms to the far corner and entered the luggage store shop, and walked up to the desk.

'Good morning, I've booked my suitcase in to be stored,' he said in a near perfect neutral English accent while showing the woman on the desk the booking reference on his phone.

'Certainly, sir, and that's for up to twenty-four hours,' she replied with a smile.

'Yes, I've had to get an earlier train, so my colleague will pick it up later today.'

'No problem, sir, just make sure they have a copy of the booking receipt so we can release the bag to them.'

'Of course, thank you very much,' Johnson said, wheeling the case around to her.

He looked her straight in the eye, keeping her focus on him as he twisted the alcohol wipe tucked in his palm around the handle of the suitcase to remove any prints or DNA before handing it over. Johnson left the luggage store and the suitcase containing the cleaned guns and the sterilised uniform he'd used on the Nova South job packed tightly beneath a bunch of clothes purchased from a charity shop. As he walked across the station, he sent the booking receipt with the message.

Baggage dropped, our business is concluded. The final payment is now due.

It took less than thirty seconds for a reply to come back.

Payment will be made to your specified account within the hour.

As soon as he'd read the message, Johnson pulled the SIM card from the phone and broke it in half, discarding it in the nearest bin before snapping the flip phone in two and depositing the pieces in another bin. While continuing to walk, he pulled out a new burner phone from his jacket pocket and turned it on as he headed for the Eurostar platforms.

Just under three hours later, Johnson stepped off the Eurostar train and made his way out of the Gare du Nord train station into the chilly Parisian night air. He walked for around half an hour until he reached the small boutique hotel he'd booked using the new phone during the journey.

Johnson checked in using the name and passport that matched his disguise, paying in cash before heading up to the specific room he'd requested. Once inside, he double locked the door and wedged the chair by the dressing table under the handle.

The room hadn't changed a bit since the last time he'd been there. That was three years ago when he was an asset working for the CIA, sent to assassinate a politician for some reason that was above his pay grade to know. Just pull the trigger, do your job and go home. Johnson shook the memory away and opened the curtains. He looked out over a flat roof just below the window, moonlight reflecting off a steel fire escape on the far side - his means for a quick escape should anyone come looking for him. He undid the latch and opened the window a crack, ready for a quick push to get out fast if he needed to. Turning back into the room, he slid the rucksack off his back and placed it on the left side of the bed before removing his jacket and placing it beside the rucksack.

Johnson headed into the ensuite bathroom. He looked at the reflection in the mirror over the sink, studying the old man looking back at him. Grabbing a towel, he wet a corner under the tap and dabbed it on his eyes and around his mouth until the prosthetic glue loosened. Putting the towel down, he undid his shirt and pulled the full head mask up and off his head. He looked up at the reflection of his real self, his hair soaked with sweat that trickled down his face. Placing the mask on top of the towel rail, he cupped his hands and washed his face. After using the towel to dry himself, Johnson smoothed his hair down and did the buttons up on his shirt before heading back into the bedroom. He put the mask inside the rucksack, then picked his jacket up and put it back on. After turning the little bedside lamp on, he clicked the main light off and lay down on the right side of the bed, fully clothed, nearest to the open window. Resting his head on the pillow, Johnson closed his eyes and breathed deeply, listening to the sounds of the room. He eventually allowed himself to sleep, but not deeply. Tomorrow, he would take a coach into Belgium before taking a flight to Marco Polo Airport, Italy, a short drive from there, and he would be in his home just outside the quiet town of Punta Sabbioni, Venice. Only then would he allow himself to sleep deeply.

CHAPTER 29

Silus Montague sat in his oak panelled office, flicking through the morning's news and social media posts to read about the murder of the National Cyber Security Centre's CEO, Giles Wright, by the terrorist group Genesis UK. He put his mug of coffee down still half full, the knots in his stomach stopping him from finishing.

Fucking Birchwood, what the hell have you done now?

His mind spun with sensory overload from the news on the screen. What would happen to him if his part in all this came out? And how was he going to keep control over Sebastian, Tobias and Rachael once they saw what Birchwood had done in the name of Genesis UK?

I'll talk to them separately, that's it. Split them up and it'll be easier to convince them that this was a necessary action for the benefit of the cause.

Silus didn't get a chance to implement his plan. The door burst open, making him physically jump up out of the chair. Sebastian stormed in angrily, followed by Rachael, her eyes blazing furiously. Tobias followed behind them, looking nervously at Montague from behind the other two.

'What the fuck, Professor?' Sebastian shouted, waving a

newspaper angrily at Silus before smacking it down on the table.

'Now hang on, calm down,' Montague said, moving around the table towards the door. He peered out into the empty corridor, closing it before turning back to the three students with his hands raised to pacify them.

'Calm down? Calm down? They're calling us a terrorist group, murderers! Who the fuck does this guy think he is? We are in charge of Genesis UK. No one consulted us about this. This guy's ruining everything. They're calling us murderers, for fuck's sake.'

'Just calm down, Sebastian, what's happened had to happen. There was no time to consult you. Action had to be taken,' Montague said, his mind spinning as he stalled for the answer to calm the situation.

'Go on then, why? Why did this have to happen? Why should we trust this man we've never met?' said Rachael, moving beside Sebastian.

'Why? Er, you trust me, don't you? Have I ever steered you wrong?' Montague said, his voice building in false confidence as he straightened to stand tall. 'The CEO of the NCSC, Giles Wright, found out about us. He was on his way to an emergency meeting to reveal what he knew. Our benefactor risked everything, his career, his freedom, even his life to remove Giles Wright and protect your identity. You should thank him, not condemn him,' Silus finished confidently, almost convincing himself the lie he spun was real.

The three students were stunned into silence, lost for words for a moment, until Sebastian finally spoke.

'We need to send a message today. Something big, something to say what we're about. We are not terrorists.'

'Yes, that's good, Sebastian. That's exactly what we need to do. Silence will just give fuel to the media's portrayal of Genesis UK,' Montague replied, happy that the focus was shifting away from yesterday's attack.

'And we want to meet the benefactor. We need to tell him we appreciate what he has done for us, but we decide what happens, not him.'

'Yes, Sebastian, leave it with me. I will talk to him and arrange a meeting,' agreed Montague, not looking forward to explaining the student's demands to Birchwood.

When the three finally left, Montague moved back around the desk and slumped into his chair, exhausted. He reached for the drawer on one side of the desk and slid it open, pulling out a bottle of Gaviscon, glugging the thick liquid down to quell the nervous acid building in his stomach. He put the bottle back in the drawer and slammed it shut, taking a few deep breaths while he rubbed his belly. Picking up the phone, Montague unlocked it, his finger shaking as it hovered over the contact for Birchwood. Try as he might, he couldn't bring himself to press the call button. He took a couple of deep breaths and put the phone back down. He needed some time to think the conversation through before he tapped the call button and faced Birchwood with the student's demands to meet him.

CHAPTER 30

Birchwood entered the Cabinet Office buildings in Whitehall. His friend Martin Webster, the Minister for Security, met him and escorted him through security and away down a long corridor.

'Are we all set?' Birchwood said in a hushed voice.

'I've had words with the PM, and after Giles Wright's death and the disappearance of Scott Miller, he's open to the discussion of scrapping Ironclad and commissioning Project Spearhead,' Webster said, leaning across to Birchwood to keep his voice a whisper.

'And this Simon character?'

'Don't worry about Simon. I sold the PM on the idea that we need an open and transparent investigation, one we can use to our political advantage with the media when we shut Genesis UK down. He's given me full control of the investigation into Genesis UK. Simon's Department D was created to covertly stamp out international threats. Under the radar, it has no place in this investigation. Genesis UK is a national threat, not an international one,' Webster said with a smile of satisfaction on his face.

'I'm impressed. I didn't think you'd be able to pull it off.'

'Well, there's an election in May and we're down on the polls. If I end this Genesis situation quickly and announce that Project Spearhead will protect us from future attacks, we all come out smelling of roses.'

'If you help me get Project Spearhead commissioned, I'm sure I can help you with Genesis UK,' Birchwood said, just as they reached the Cabinet Office Briefing Rooms or COBR, as it is more commonly known.

Webster smiled back at Birchwood before knocking on the door and entering when it was opened for him.

'Prime Minister, ministers, you remember Alfred Birchwood from Birchwood Technologies.'

'Yes, thank you for coming at such short notice. Please, please take a seat.'

'Thank you, Prime Minister, please don't mention it. I was appalled at the news of Giles Wright, Christian Flowers and James Howman's deaths. I knew them all personally, it's a terrible loss to the country,' said Birchwood, doing his best to look genuinely upset.

'Yes of course, which is why we wish to discuss Project Spearhead.'

'Project Spearhead is 100% complete and ready to implement. It's been running at Birchwood Technologies for two years without a single breach,' Birchwood said with supreme confidence.

'Let's not get ahead of ourselves, Mr Birchwood. We are also exploring the possibility of using a third party to upgrade the Ironclad system,' the PM said, looking across at the Secretary of State for his input.

'And that would be Scott Miller, I presume, and where is Mr Miller?' Birchwood said, throwing the PM off guard.

'Mr Miller is currently missing, held by person or persons as yet not identified.'

'Well, one would hope that nothing bad has happened to him. After all, it would be very unfortunate and extremely difficult to explain to the British public if one put all one's eggs in one basket only to find someone has taken the basket away. Your choice, of course, but I'm here and I can implement Project Spearhead immediately.'

The PM was about to answer when the phone in the middle of the desk rang.

'Yes, right, I see. Put it on the screen,' he said, putting the phone down to point at the big screen at the end of the room.

The screen burst into life to show an artificial intelligence deepfake version of himself standing at the podium outside of Number 10 Downing Street, a Genesis UK banner strung across the brickwork behind him. The hacked-in broadcast showed him apologising for the failure of his party before announcing that Genesis UK was the only party that could save the country and give people the future they deserved. He went on to explain that the media had wrongly portrayed Genesis UK as terrorists when they were really visionaries, determined to stand up against the establishment to make a better future for all.

'What channels are they broadcasting on?' the PM said down the phone. 'What, all of them? How is that possible?' He continued as the broadcast ended with a support Genesis UK message in big lettering across the screen. The second it disappeared and the scheduled programme came back on air, the power went out as Genesis UK hacked the National Grid for a second time. The PM looked around slowly, putting the phone back on its cradle as the dim emergency lighting reflected his mood.

'Let's talk figures, Mr Birchwood,' the PM finally said.

'Very good, Prime Minister,' Birchwood said, putting his briefcase on the table in front of him. The building's generator kicked in a second later, putting power back into the room, illuminating the proposals in Birchwood's hand as he passed them around the table.

CHAPTER 31

After a restless night, Danny paced around the house like a bear with a sore head. The frustration of waiting for some sliver of information to act on was driving him insane. Nikki wasn't much better. It was difficult to know what was worse, worrying about her brother, or worrying about limits her husband would go to get him back. Danny's phone finally rang, shattering the tension in the air and making Nikki jump.

'Good morning, Daniel,' came Simon's voice on the other end.

'What have you got for me, Simon?' Danny said impatiently back.

'Mmm. To the point, as ever. Special Branch has found the narrowboat, it's been abandoned in Alperton, near Ealing Road.'

'Any clues?' Danny said impatiently, interrupting him as he spoke.

'No, nothing of any use. The boat's been cleaned with bleach from head to toe. Special Branch has the local police checking the canal path and local area in case he dumped the uniform and weapons from the Nova attack. I doubt they'll find anything, my best guess is he headed straight to Alperton Tube station and on to god knows where. They're checking flights out of Heathrow Airport in case he took a flight out of the country, but as they only have a general description, it's not looking hopeful. Anyway, on to other news, I have found your Deliveroo delivery man, and he did indeed take a photograph of the van that took Scott. We tracked its movement through traffic division's ANPR cameras to Birchanger Green Services on the M11 near Stansted Airport, where we believe they changed the registration plates in the car park as the cameras didn't pick the reg up as it left. They didn't help anyway. The plates used at Scott's apartment were false. They belong to a Mercedes Vito van in Birmingham.'

'Damn, any other leads?' Danny said.

'Patience, Daniel. I have my people going through hours of camera footage from all routes leading away from the service station, looking at every grey Ford Transit van that passes. It will take a little time to check the owners and narrow the list down, but I will let you know as soon as we get a result. Now, in the meantime I have narrowed the list of fixers close enough to London and with the necessary contacts to supply our American friend down to two. I thought you might like to check them out while we work on the location of the van,' Simon said, his manner light and cheery.

'Ok, let me have them,' Danny replied.

'You already do, dear boy. Speak to you later.'

With that Simon hung up.

'What did he say? Does he know where Scott is?' said Nikki, desperate for good news.

'Not yet, but he's getting closer,' Danny replied, getting to his feet to move swiftly past Nikki into the hall.

There was nothing sticking through the letterbox or on the doormat, so Danny opened the front door to see nothing outside. As he closed it, he could feel a through-draught blowing past his ear from the kitchen behind him. Turning, he headed to the kitchen with Nikki following him with a puzzled look on her face. The back door was ajar, still swinging in the breeze. An A4 manila envelope sat on the kitchen table. Danny stepped outside and looked down the passage that led from the back of the houses to the front, but nobody was in sight.

He returned to the kitchen where Nikki was holding the envelope with a worried look on her face.

'It's ok, it's just Simon's idea of a joke.'

She breathed a sigh of relief and handed the envelope to Danny. Flipping the seal up, Danny pulled the papers from inside and placed them on the table before spreading them out. There were two personnel files complete with police arrest mugshots and long distance surveillance shots taken with a powerful camera lens. The pictures were a little fuzzy, but still clear enough to recognise the suspects if you saw them in the flesh.

'Who are they?' Nikki said, standing behind Danny as he sat studying them.

'Fixers, one of these two supplied our killer with the uniforms and guns to pull off the Nova South attack,' Danny said, picking up one with a mugshot on top.

'Which one do you think it is?' Nikki said, reading the criminal record of the one in Danny's hand.

'I don't know. This one is the closest. I'll start with him,' Danny said, getting out of the chair.

'Wait, I'm coming with you,' Nikki answered quickly, standing in Danny's way.

'No, you're not,' Danny replied, frowning.

'Yes, I am,' Nikki said, refusing to stand aside.

They stood staring at each other until Danny finally gave in. He reached behind his back and pulled out his Glock 17 and handed it to her.

'Fine, but you're staying in the car, no arguments. I'm going to get my other gun,' Danny said, heading upstairs to his black holdall hidden in the bottom of the wardrobe.

'Yes dear,' Nikki smiled, picking up her handbag from the back of a kitchen chair and slipping the gun inside.

CHAPTER 32

'Oi, Matt, gloves on, and all litter goes in the black bag,' Nick Temple shouted, entering the remote farmhouse on the outskirts of Cambridge to find the kitchen in a mess.

'Alright, alright,' Matt grumbled back.

'No, it's not fucking alright, you keep your fucking gloves on, overalls on and hat on, we leave no forensic evidence when we go, got it? None. That includes your fucking sweaty fingerprints on that Twix wrapper. You got it, you idiot?' Temple shouted, picking up the bin bag and shaking it in front of him until he put the chocolate bar wrapper inside.

'I say, bad guys, hello, anyone?' came a faint cry from somewhere above them.

'What the fuck does he want now?' moaned the third man on the team.

'It's your turn, Darren. If I have to deal with him again I'm going to fucking do him.'

'Oh for fuck's sake,' said Darren, getting up out of his chair to pull the balaclava rolled up on top of his head down to cover his face.

'Darren,' Temple said before he left the room.

'Yeah?'

'Go easy, the boss needs him alive ok?' ordered Temple.

'Ok, ok I got it.'

Darren stepped into the hall and made his way upstairs. The farmhouse was dark inside, the abundance of oak on the stairs and the panelling and doors adding to the gloom. It was also cold and damp from not being lived in for several years. A smell of musty decay hung in the air. He moved along the landing to a room at the front of the house and turned the key. Unlocking the heavy oak door, he pushed it open and stared at Scott sitting in a chair in the middle of the room, his arms crossed as he looked angrily back at his captor.

'Good god, this is intolerable. How long are you infernal people going to keep me here tied up like an animal?' Scott said, raising his voice and shaking his leg so that the chain and padlock around his ankle rattled all the way to the thick wooden leg of an old four poster bed.

'If you don't stop your whining, you posh prick, I'm going to kill you painfully with my bare hands,' Darren growled back.

'No, you won't. If you wanted me dead you would have done it back at my apartment, with no kidnapping and no balaclavas to hide your ugly faces. You're just the hired help, an obedient dog who does as he's told. Now run along like a good boy and fetch me a drink and some food.'

Behind the balaclava, Darren's face went scarlet with rage. He stepped forward and punched Scott in the stomach with all his might, knocking him backwards off his seat to land flat on his back, coughing and spluttering. Still in a rage, Darren moved in to finish Scott off. As he stood over him, the unmistakable click-clack of a handgun slide being pulled back sounded before Darren felt the pressure of cold steel on the back of his head.

'I told you we need him alive. Now go downstairs and cool off before I put a bullet in your head,' growled Temple.

Darren didn't move for a while, rage and reasoning battling with each other until he finally relented, backed away until he left the room. Temple tucked the gun into the back of his trousers and picked the chair up, placing it upright before helping Scott up off the floor and dumping him on the seat as he tried to catch his breath.

'I'd advise you not to antagonise him again. The next time I might not be here to stop him. I'll get you a drink and something to eat,' Temple said calmly, his eyes staring at Scott through the balaclava.

Scott just stared back, breathing heavily. He watched Temple leave the room before holding his stomach and groaning in pain.

CHAPTER 33

isten to me, you old pervert, I don't give a shit how much that little bunch of juvenile, eco warrior, fucking weirdo geniuses protest about what I'm doing. Dealing with them is your job. That's what I'm paying a lot of money for. If this all goes wrong I'll make sure you go down for this and all your other nasty little indiscretions, and you know what they do to paedophiles like you in prison. Now, we're one step away from getting the contract for Project Spearhead signed off. I just need one more push to get the last members of the security council on my side and it's a done deal. I've sent you the details of what I want and you better get it done. Don't screw this up, Silus,' Birchwood barked down the phone.

'Yes, of course, I understand that, but I need to give them something. They want to meet you. They want to know who this mysterious benefactor from inside the government is. If they don't get what they want, I'm not sure they'll do what you want,' Montague said, bracing himself for Birchwood's response.

There was a long silence while Birchwood thought the

situation through, the tension making Montague feel physically sick.

'Ok, I'll give them a meeting. Just get them to do this one last thing for me. I'll arrange the time and place once I have Project Spearhead in the bag. You will get your money and a flight out of the country with a new identity as promised, and they will take the fall for the terrorist attacks and deaths. Do you think you can handle all that?' Birchwood finally said, his voice suspiciously calm.

'Yes Alfred.'

'You damn well better, Silus,' Birchwood said, his voice returning to a shout before he hung up.

Silus Montague opened the message that arrived in the secure internet portal a second later. His face fell as he read it. He let out a stressed sigh before deleting it and shutting the portal down. He logged into the university network and checked room availability before booking the one he wanted for a three-hour slot. Turning the computer off, he picked up his phone and typed out a message with shaking fingers and sent it to three contacts.

I.T.1.23. Thirty minutes.

Montague took a few minutes to compose himself and think about what he was going to say to Tobias, Rachael and Sebastian before leaving his office in the 500-year-old four-storey college building. He headed down the stone staircase and out through a heavy oak door into the courtyard, smiling and nodding to students as he went. He took the centuries old flagstone path through the centre of the immaculately manicured lawns, exiting the courtyard through the north exit. After a short walk through the college grounds, Montague entered the technology building, heading down the corridor to IT suite I.T.1.23. He could hear raised voices before he got to the door. When he opened it, Rachael and

Sebastian were face to face arguing, while Tobias stood behind them looking like he might burst into tears at any moment.

'No, fuck you, Sebastian, this has got way out of control. It's not what I signed up for. I wanted to change the world for good, not get tarnished as a terrorist,' Rachael shouted.

'And there's only one way to do that, or are you that stupid you think that a few parlour tricks, turn the power on and off, fuck with their phones and piss about with the traffic lights are going to make them roll over and play dead? Extreme change takes extreme action, and if a few people get hurt in the process, then so be it,' Sebastian barked back.

'Hey, hey, come on, let's calm it down. You've come so far and the end is in sight. I come bearing great news,' Montague said, stopping them in their tracks.

'What news?' Sebastian said, watching Montague shut and lock the door.

'Our friend in government says he has growing support for Genesis UK with other political members. Many are pledging their support for a reformation of government. And that's not all. He wants a meeting with you.'

Sebastian's eyes shone at the news. 'When?'

'Soon, Sebastian, he still has a few to persuade. Timing is everything. He needs you to do one last thing, to show that the present government has no control over their country. Do this for him and he'll meet you and share his plans to come out of the shadows and move Genesis UK into power,' Montague said, his words convincing as he watched the students looking back at him with trusting eyes.

'What do you think, Professor, can we trust him?' Rachael said when he'd finished.

'Of course, I know it's a lot to take in, and it's hard to trust when you don't even know who he is. But you trust me, don't you?'

'Yes, of course,' Rachael said.

'Absolutely,' Sebastian chipped in, while Tobias nodded his head nervously behind them.

'Good, well I trust him and you will too once you meet him.'

'What is it he wants us to do?' Sebastian said.

Montague looked at their faces, trusting, loving him like a father, hanging on his every word.

CHAPTER 34

'Nice area,' Nikki said as Danny drove the car under an arch into a large courtyard, parking the car in a space with a burnt-out car to their left and a dumped old sofa on their right.

'You wanted to come,' Danny said, giving her a grin before looking out the window at the four-storey concrete jungle of council flats surrounding them on all sides.

'Isn't it a bit, er, public for someone who supplies guns and explosives?' Nikki said, noticing people coming and going from the surrounding flats and a group of youths eyeing them cautiously from the scruffy patch of green space that passed as a park in the middle of the flats.

'Nah, it's ideal. He can hide in plain sight and there are plenty of watchful eyes to warn him if the authorities enter the estate. He's probably watching us now,' Danny said, opening the door to get out. 'Stay here,' Danny added, giving Nikki a look that showed he meant it.

'Ok, be careful,' she reluctantly replied.

'I always am,' Danny said, pausing before he shut the door. 'You might want to lock the door after me,' he added with a grin.

Nikki pulled a face and patted the handbag slung across her shoulder with the gun inside.

'Ok, ok, just saying,' Danny added before shutting the door and heading towards a stairwell leading to the fourth floor and the address on Simon's file for the known arms dealer Micky Mitchell.

Nikki's phone buzzed as she sat waiting. She took it out to find it was just a work related e-mail. While she was busy typing a reply, there was a dull thud from the rear of the car. She twisted in her seat to look out through the rear window. When she couldn't see anything, she ducked her head down so she could see down the side of the car in the wing mirror. The wheel of a bicycle on its side was visible, still spinning gently in a circle as it lay behind the car. A second later, a boy struggled to his feet and hobbled around, holding his face in pain.

'Oh God,' Nikki said, getting out of the car with the phone still in her hand. 'Are you alright?' she called out, moving to the back of the car, concerned for the boy.

He didn't answer, just shook his head and stood bent over with his back to her.

'Just take it easy, here, let me see.'

He slowly stood upright, dropping his hands as he turned to show a menacing grin. Nikki backed up a step and bumped into someone else. She whipped around to see a much larger youth staring coldly from under a pulled-up hoodie, two more of his gang standing behind him dressed in similar attire.

'Nice car, lady, cost a pretty penny I'll bet. Now give us your phone and bag. Come on, you don't want me to cut you,' he said, a large knife sliding out from the sleeve of his baggy hoodie until the hand that gripped it tightly appeared from beneath the material.

Nikki kept calm, feigning fear as she handed her phone towards him with a shaky left hand. He stepped forward, reaching out to grab it, a surprised look spreading across his face as she pulled it back and kicked out with all her might, the toe of her pointy boot striking him firmly in the balls. As he doubled up, winded, Nikki powered a right hook into the side of his face, twisting the knuckles as they made contact for a more effective punch. He went down, dropping the knife as he fell. The hours Danny had spent teaching her Krav Maga and other fighting techniques coming into their own.

Nikki dropped the phone on the roof of the BMW and twisted around to grab the youth standing behind her by the shoulder of his jacket. Lifting and bending her leg, she pulled herself towards him and drove her knee violently into his ribs, cracking one before dropping her leg and snapping her elbow up so the hard bony part smacked the youth under the chin. Teeth cracked as his mouth snapped shut, his head whipped back and his body followed as he fell back over his bicycle, rolling off awkwardly off it to curl up in pain on the tarmac.

'That's it, lady, I'm really going to fuck you up now,' growled one of the two gang members still standing, a large commando knife glinting in his hand, a similar one held in the hand of the thug standing behind him.

Before he could make another step forward, she flipped her bag open and pulled the Glock handgun out, locking her arm out straight in front of her so the barrel pointed between the youth's eyes.

'Go ahead, try to fuck me up. I dare you,' she said angrily, watching the colour drain from the youth's face.

'Ok cool it, lady, we're going, ok,' he said as quickly as he could, his voice shaky and eyes wide with fear as he looked down the barrel of the gun.

Giving Nikki a wide berth, they picked up their two fallen gang members and scooted off as fast as they could, disappearing into the maze of alleys and stairwells that made up the estate.

Nikki looked around the flats surrounding her, amazed that no one either saw what had happened or wanted to get involved enough to help her. Placing the gun back into her bag, she picked her phone off the roof of the car and got back inside, hoping Danny wouldn't be much longer.

CHAPTER 35

Danny reached the fourth floor and headed down the long concrete landing with a three-foot-high brick wall on one side that looked out onto the other blocks of flats forming a square around the carpark and balding patch of grass at its centre. Rows of front doors and kitchen windows looked back at him from all sides. Danny picked out Micky Mitchell's flat up ahead without having to see the number. Three CCTV cameras looked out from above the door, one covering Danny as he approached, while the other cameras pointed at the two entry points into the estate. Danny stopped by the door, looking at the locked metal gate in front of it and the metal bars fitted over the kitchen window next to him. Smiling at the camera, Danny reached forward and poked the intercom buzzer with his finger.

'What the fuck do you want?' came a crackly angry voice over the speaker.

'I was told you could get me something very specific for a job.'

'Well, you were told wrong then. Now fuck off.'

Danny reached inside his jacket pocket and pulled out a

fat roll of fifty-pound notes and twiddled it between his thumb and index finger at the camera above his head. The sound of bolts sliding back on the door could be heard before it opened just far enough to see Micky Mitchell's face looking over a steel chain.

'Who told you about me?' he said, still suspicious.

'The American,' Danny said, watching the man's face closely.

There it was, a moment of confusion over 'the American'. He tried to hide it, his eyes fixed greedily on the roll of fifties as he lied to Danny.

'Yeah, the American, of course. Come in and we'll talk.'

While Micky Mitchell closed the door enough to unhook the chain, Danny was walking away. He opened the door and looked through the metal gate as he jiggled the key in the padlock to unlock it.

'Hey, where the fuck are you going?' he shouted after him.

Ignoring him, Danny took the stairs back down to the ground level and crossed the courtyard to the car. He opened the door and jumped in, looking across at Nikki as he started the engine.

'Any good?'

'Nah, he didn't know him. You been alright?'

'Yeah, I've been getting to know the locals. What now?' Nikki smiled back.

'Er, time's getting on, I say we head home and see if Simon's had any more leads on the van that took Scott. We'll check out the fixer in Tilbury tomorrow.'

'Ok,' Nikki said, placing her hand on Danny's arm.

He looked down and spotted her red knuckles, then up with questions written across his face.

'They were rude,' she smiled back.

'I hope you taught them some manners,' Danny replied, reversing the car out between the burnt-out car and dumped sofa before driving under the arch and out of the estate.

'I think they got the message,' Nikki said, putting her hand lightly on the back of Danny's neck as he drove.

CHAPTER 36

'B772 requesting permission to take off.'

'Good morning, B772, you are cleared for take off.'

'Thank you, control, B772 preparing to take off.'

Warren allowed his eyes to glance out the window of Heathrow's control tower to see the British Airways flight B772 accelerate down the runway. He didn't bother to watch as its wheels left the ground. The wonder of these massive hunks of metal leaving the earth had long since held any magic. This was Heathrow. There was no time for sightseeing. A plane took off every forty seconds.

'This is flight A388 requesting permission to take off.'

'Good morning, A388, you are cleared for take off.'

Radio talk from one of his colleagues made Warren glance over while he waited for flight A388's response.

'Flight B78X, come in, please,'

'Problem, Philip?' Warren said to him while muting his mic.

'Control, this is flight A388 requesting permission to take off.'

'Control to flight A388, you are still cleared for take off,'

Warren repeated, looking out the window to see the aircraft still sitting at the end of the runway.

'Flight B78X. Come in, please. You need to alter your course to 172. I repeat, alter course to 172,' Philip said, turning to Warren when he didn't get a response. 'Hold your flight, Warren. B78X is heading straight for the northern runway and they're not responding.'

'Flight A388, maintain your position, you are not cleared for take off. I repeat, do not take off.'

The tension grew in the control tower and the supervisor moved across to see what was going on.

'Thank you, control, this is A388 taking off. You have a good day too.'

'Christ, they're heading straight for each other,' the supervisor said, looking at the radar screen.

'This is Flight B78X. Thank you, control, we have a visual on the alternate runway.'

'Who the hell are they talking to?' Philip said, trying to reach B78X again.

'Oh my god, someone's hijacked the transmissions. Keep trying them while I call it in.'

'This is B78X approaching run— Christ, there's a plane taking off. Aborting landing, come on, pull up, pull up.'

'Jesus, a plane coming straight for us,' came the simultaneous radio message from flight A388.

They watched helplessly from the control tower as A388 took off and banked hard right, while B78X pulled up, the two planes missing each other by metres. As they breathed a sigh of relief, a voice came over everyone's headsets.

'This is Genesis UK. The aviation industry equates to 2.5% of all global CO2 emissions. This was just a warning. We will not just stand by and watch the destruction of the planet. There is a better way. Genesis UK is the only future.'

As soon as the message finished, their ears filled with urgent radio traffic from a dozen or more planes, all backed up in the stack above them, waiting to land, and parked along the tarmac, waiting to take off.

'Close the airport down, close it all down now. No one takes off until the CAA gives us the go ahead. Land those low on fuel and divert the rest to Gatwick, or City airport, or Stansted,' shouted the supervisor, tapping the emergency contact button on his phone to report the attack.

CHAPTER 37

Nikki came back from the high street with coffee and Danish pastries to find Danny still pacing around the house like a caged animal.

'Any news from Simon?'

'He's getting closer. They've been running checks on all the vans that were near Birchanger Services on the day Scott disappeared. The list is getting shorter, and he hopes to have more information later today.'

'Ok, so what's the plan then? What are we doing?' Nikki said, handing him a coffee and a cinnamon swirl.

'I'm going to check out the other guy on Simon's list of fixers. You're staying here,' Danny said forcibly.

'Oh no no no, we went through this yesterday. I'm coming with you,' Nikki replied, her arms crossed with a don't-mess-with-me look on her face.

'Yeah, and look what happened yesterday, you nearly got shish kebabed by Boyz n the Hood. You're not coming, no way, end of conversation,' Danny growled, his words coming out angrier than he intended them to.

'And I dealt with them perfectly well without your help. So you can shove your poor defenceless female attitude where the sun doesn't shine, because I'm coming. Got it, yes way, end of conversation,' Nikki fired back, the two of them looking angrily into each other's eyes.

Danny broke the stalemate first by stomping off to the front door. Nikki's face dropped, thinking he was going to walk out on her until he opened it and turned back.

'Well come on then if you're coming,' he said, his face softening and his mouth curling up into a grin.

Nikki immediately changed from annoyed to excited. She grabbed her handbag with the gun still in it and hurried towards Danny, kissing him on the cheek as she passed him.

Danny rolled his eyes as he shut the front door, walking to the car and his waiting wife. They drove out of London and headed around the M25, turning off at Thurrock before heading to the address in Simon's file for Robson Mann. They had to park on the road as the address turned out to be a very unassuming 1950s three bedroom house on the end of a block of four houses facing onto a lawned area with an identical block of houses on the opposite side. Danny got out of the car without saying a word.

'Oh, I'll just stay here then,' Nikki muttered, watching Danny walk around the car.

To her surprise, he stopped at the passenger door and opened it for her.

'Come on, I need backup,' he said, chuckling.

Nikki didn't need telling twice. She got out and followed Danny toward the house.

'You sure this is the right address?' Nikki said, looking at the neat little front garden with a perfectly manicured lawn surrounded by colourful flower beds and a freshly varnished bench placed under the front window with floral net curtains hanging inside.

'Er, number fifty-six, yeah, that's what it says in the file,' said Danny, shrugging and opening the garden gate before walking up to the door.

He pressed the doorbell and waited. Eventually, a shadow appeared through the frosted glass as it shuffled towards the door. When the lock clicked and the door swung open, an elderly woman looked back at them with a polite smile on her face.

'Hello, can I help you?'

'Er, sorry, we're looking for Robson, Robson Mann?' Danny said.

'I'm afraid he's not here, my dear,' the old lady said.

'Do you know where we might find him, Mrs…?'

'Mann, but call me Irene, dear. I'm his mother. Are you friends of his?' she asked, still smiling, but guarding her answers.

'Yes, I've been away for a while and just wanted to catch up,' Danny said, keeping his answer light.

'Oh, you're one of his friends from prison. I'm so glad you're out and on the straight and narrow.'

Caught by surprise, Danny just nodded and smiled while Nikki took his arm and stood next to him.

'And with such a lovely girlfriend,' Irene said, looking at Nikki. 'He'll be down at his father's old lockup on Dock Road. He's always tinkering about down there. I can call him if you like?'

'No, that's fine. I'll pop down and surprise him. What number did you say it was, Irene?' said Danny, with him and Nikki giving her their friendliest smiles.

'It's number seven, next door to Milton's Garage.'

'Thank you very much, Mrs Mann,' Danny said, leaving her to walk back to the car before driving the short distance to Dock Road.

CHAPTER 38

'Surely this can't be the guy. He lives with his mum,' said Nikki.

'Stranger things have happened. It's a good cover and he's been to prison for arms dealing,' Danny said, slowing down as he drove past Milton's Garage. He turned in his seat to look through the open gate at the scruffy storage unit with a blue Nissan Micra parked outside.

Danny spun the car around at the end of the road, pulling over a little short of the storage unit.

'So how are we going to play this?' Nikki said, suddenly feeling a little out of her depth.

'Now, don't take this the wrong way, love, but I'm going in alone. He's going to be jumpy enough as it is and he could be armed. If we both go in asking questions we're going to get nowhere.'

'Ok, be careful,' replied Nikki, knowing he was right.

Danny smiled at her and leaned over to give her a kiss.

'Give me your gun,' he said, pulling away to reach behind and pull his own gun from the back of his jeans. Twisting around, Danny reached into the footwell behind his seat and grabbed the black holdall taken from under the bedroom wardrobe. He unzipped it, giving a flash of the automatic rifle and spare magazines before placing his own and Nikki's guns inside and zipping it up.

'I didn't realise you brought that with you. What are you doing?' Nikki said, puzzled.

'He's an arms dealer, right? Well, I'm going to sell him some arms,' Danny said, giving her a wink before getting out of the car.

Taking a deep breath, Danny walked along the side of the overgrown concrete block wall and through the open gate. He crossed the small yard to the metal door of the works unit and rapped his knuckles loudly on its rusty surface. Ten seconds later, the small square hatch slid to one side and a pair of eyes stared suspiciously at him.

'Who the fuck are you?' Robson snarled.

'The big Irishman you were in Belmarsh with said you'd be interested in some merchandise that's come into my possession,' Danny said, twisting slightly to show the holdall slung over his shoulder.

'What Irishman?' said Robson, his eyes flicking from Danny to the holdall, to the road beyond the yard then back to Danny.

'Fucked if I know. Patrick, I think. He was pissed as a parrot and started a fight. The silly bastard trashed the pub and got arrested just after he told me,' Danny said matter of fact.

'Fuck off, I don't know any Irishmen,' Robson said, but he didn't shut the hatch.

'Ok fine, I'll take these somewhere else,' Danny said, turning to walk away, purposely showing the holdall as he headed off.

'Hang on. What have you got?' Robson called after him, his curiosity piqued.

Danny stood still with his back to Robson, a smile spreading across his face before he turned and walked back to the door. He looked around like he was worried about prying eyes, then unzipped the holdall just far enough to give a fleeting glimpse of the two Glock 17s and the AR-15 semiautomatic rifle before zipping it back up.

'Put the bag down and lift your top,' Robson demanded.

'What?'

'Lift your fucking top. I want to see if you're wearing a wire.'

Danny let out a sigh then did as Robson said.

'Turn around.'

'Come on, man, give me a break,' Danny said, turning a full 360 so Robson could see his bare torso all the way around.

'Ok, wait there,' Robson said, shutting the hatch before the metal scraping sound of the locking bar being removed sounded through the door.

When it opened, a scruffy Robson in dirty jeans and creased sweatshirt beckoned him in, shutting the door and sliding the locking bar in place behind them.

'Sorry about that. You can't be too careful you know. Can I get you anything, tea, coffee?' he said, his demeanour completely changing to warm and friendly.

'Coffee, one sugar,' Danny said, playing along.

Robson clicked the dirty white kettle on and came back to Danny while it boiled. 'So let's have a look at what you've got,' he said with a greedy glint in his eyes.

Danny placed the holdall onto an empty flight case in the middle of the unit and unzipped it. He placed the Glocks on its top, then took the AR-15 out, folding the stock out and clicking a magazine into it.

'Nice. What do you want for them?' Robson said, turning when the kettle boiled and clicked off to make the drinks.

Before he could move, bullets whizzed past him, obliterating the kettle, cups and tatty kitchen units in a cloud of wood, plastic and ceramic pieces, the metallic pings from the silencer still sounding loud in the confined space. Robson bent double until the shooting stopped, straightened up and patted his sweatshirt expecting to see blood and bullet holes. He looked up slowly to see Danny pointing the rifle at his head.

'The American,' Danny growled, watching for Robson's reaction at his mention.

'What American? I don't know any Americans,' Robson blurted back, but Danny had seen his eyes go wide and the split-second pause as he thought about his response.

Danny looked along the sights and squeezed off another shot, sending a bullet through the empty space of Robson's low hung jeans just below his balls. Before the tuft of denim had drifted to the floor, Robson started to talk fast.

'Stop, stop, fuck, don't shoot.'

'The American killed a very good friend of mine with a handgun that you supplied, one very similar to this one,' Danny said, putting the AR-15 down and picking up one of the Glocks. He pulled the slide back to chamber a round before walking up to Robson and placing it onto the middle of his forehead.

'He was here. Fuck, don't. The American was here. He used the name Montana. I'm sorry about your friend. What the fuck do you want me to say?' Robson blubbered, almost in tears.

'I want to know everything he said, everything he did, what he looked like. Talk,' Danny growled, his face inches away from Robson's.

'I don't know anything about him, man. A couple of weeks ago some rich dude contacted me. He wanted some explosives and got me to drop the gear off in one of those self serve locker places. A few days ago I get another message with a list of kit they want. The guy says an American called Montana will come and collect it. That's all I know.'

'That can't be it, there must be something, think,' Danny yelled while pushing the gun harder into Robson's forehead.

'A tattoo. He had a tattoo on the back of his left shoulder. I saw it when he tried the uniform on. A fucking frog, a skeleton frog holding a fucking fork.'

'A trident,' Danny growled back.

'Yeah, fucking fork, trident, whatever. It had something written underneath it.'

'What?' Danny yelled again.

'Wait, I can't think, er, something about yesterday, easy days or something.'

'The only easy day was yesterday,' Danny said, moving the gun off Robson's forehead to leave a circular imprint on his skin.

'Yeah, that was it. The only easy day was yesterday.'

'The rich guy that contacted you. What do you know about him?' Danny said, moving back to the flight case to put the Glocks in the holdall before picking the AR-15 back up.

'I don't know anything other than he was real clever with computers. That's how he contacted me. I was just sitting here, and he took my computer over. Opened up some secure message service, then made it vanish when he was done.'

'How did he pay you?'

'The first time he credited my bank account, just like that. I didn't even give him the details. No payment ID, no name, just money in the account. The second time the American gave me cash.'

Danny looked at Robson. The terrified man was telling the truth.

'It's a lot different being on the wrong end of one of these than just selling one, isn't it?' he said, still pointing the rifle at Robson.

Robson was shaking from head to toe with tears coming from his eyes as he nodded.

'You're retired as of now, you understand me?'

'Yes, yes, that's it I'm through,' Robson blubbered.

'You ever deal again, I'll know and I'll be back. There'll be no second chances. You understand me?'

'Yes, I understand, thank you.'

Danny kept pointing the rifle at him for a few more seconds just to emphasise the point, then folded the stock up and placed the rifle in the holdall. He zipped it up and slung it over his shoulder before walking over to the door. Danny lifted the bar off and opened it to walk out into the open air.

'Change your life, Robson, make your mum proud of you,' Danny shouted back as he walked across the yard and out the gate.

When he reached the car, Danny opened the boot and put the holdall inside before closing it and getting in the driving seat.

'Well,' Nikki said impatiently.

'Yeah, he was the one who supplied the American,' Danny said with his phone in his hand.

'How did it go? You didn't, er, you know,' Nikki said, not daring to say the word.

'No. I persuaded him to do the right thing, that's all.'

'Oh god, you tortured him,' Nikki gasped.

'No, I never laid a finger on him. He's fine, ok?' Danny said, rolling his eyes.

'Sorry,' Nikki said after a few seconds.

'That's alright. Just give me a minute. I've got to call this in,' Danny replied, calling Simon.

'Daniel,' Simon answered, the phone barely having a chance to ring.

'Robson Mann supplied the American, but I don't think he has anything to do with Genesis UK. I think he's just a professional gun for hire. I doubt he even knows who the client is. Whoever contacted Mann did it by taking over his computer with an untraceable message service, and whoever is funding Genesis UK is rich and very well connected.'

'Yes, quite. I do have my suspicions regarding that.'

'Martin Webster, the Minister for Security?'

'It's a possibility. He does seem to be going out of his way to keep my department out of the investigation. Did you find out anything else about our American friend?' Simon said, moving the conversation off the subject of the minister.

'Yes, he was a Navy Seal and is using the name Montana. He has a tattoo of a skeleton frog holding a trident on the back of his left shoulder with the motto, *the only easy day was yesterday* underneath it.'

'Good work, I'll have to have a quiet word with some of my contacts across the pond. We have prints and DNA. As long as the US Navy plays ball, we should get a name to put to the face.'

'Any news on the van that took Scott?'

'Yes, I have. We've narrowed it down to one van. They changed number plates at Birchanger Green Services for a second set of false plates, then continued down the M11 until Cambridge where we lost them north of the city.'

'So we don't know any more than we did yesterday,' Danny said despondently.

'On the contrary, Daniel, the van in question is of a model that only came into effect in 2019. As no van with the false plates hit any ANPR cameras leaving the area, one can assume that it reached its destination somewhere north of Cambridge. Did you know there are only twenty-three vans registered in the Cambridge area that match that model and colour? We are running background checks against all the owners while checking our list of registration plates against ones caught on traffic cameras elsewhere at the same time as our suspect vehicle, so we can eliminate them from the list. I imagine we will have a considerably shorter list of registered owners by the morning.'

'Good. I'll head to Cambridge first thing. Send me that list as soon as you can.'

'Of course,' Simon said before hanging up.

'Still no idea where Scott is,' Nikki said, worried about her brother.

'No, but we're getting closer. We just have to be patient,' said Danny, putting his arm around her. 'Come on, let's go home.'

CHAPTER 39

Scott sat in the bedroom, drumming his fingers on his leg. The boredom of being chained up in the drab bedroom with nothing to do was worse than any threat his amateur-hour captors could throw at him.

If I have to stare at this hideous wallpaper for much longer, I swear I'll go mad.

He'd kicked off his shoes ages ago and was scrunching, then stretching his toes inside his Harrods cashmere socks, a relaxation technique from one of the many classes he took at his exclusive sports club. Scott looked at the chain padlocked around his wrist, then down at his feet. A memory sparked in his head as he repeated the look from one to the other.

'Of course, why didn't I think of that before?' he muttered to himself.

Bending down, he slid a sock off his foot and held it up in front of him.

Now, let me think, how did that fellow in the YouTube video get out of those handcuffs?

Scott thought back, replaying the video in his head. Then slid the sock over his hand, tucking it under the chain around his wrist before pulling it up to his forearm. He tucked his thumb into his palm and folded the open end of the sock forward until it was both under and over the chain. Pulling the open end of the sock towards his fingers, Scott felt the chain sliding down his hand between the sock material, whilst compressing his thumb and fingers to a point where it popped over the thumb knuckle and slid off onto the floor.

'Ha, I'll be damn it works. Take that bad guys. It'll take more than that to hold Scott Miller,' Scott muttered, pleased with himself.

He quickly put his sock and shoes on, then got up out of his seat and tiptoed over to the window. The grey van sat below him on a gravel courtyard. A long dirt drive led off into woodland with no sign of a house or road anywhere close by. A fenced-in meadow sat to the left of the farmhouse with more woodland beyond it, and a large hay barn sat to the right. With thoughts of jumping down, Scott tried to open the sash window, only to find it screwed shut. Deciding not to risk breaking it and alerting his captors, Scott backed up and tiptoed over to the bedroom door. He reached for the handle and twisted it slowly until the latch drew into the door and it popped open. Pulling it, Scott stuck his head through the gap and looked out onto an empty square landing.

So far so good. Keep calm, Scotty boy, keep calm.

Looking like he'd had some sort of accident, Scott did his best attempt at walking silently across the landing towards the top of the stairs. He held his breath and wobbled precariously on tiptoes when a floorboard creaked under foot.

Damn and blast it.

Nothing happened, no shouts, and no one came charging up the stairs. Scott exhaled deeply and regained his composure before easing his foot down onto the first step. He continued down the stairs until he could duck down low enough to see the downstairs hallway and front door. A door was slightly ajar to a room on the right and he could hear voices in conversation coming from within, but they were too muffled and quiet for Scott to tell what they were saying. Focusing on the front door, Scott tiptoed down the stairs until his feet touched the tiled hall floor.

Hold your nerve, old man, just a little bit further.

Scooting across the hall, Scott grabbed the ancient metal doorknob, turning and pulling it. The door wouldn't budge.

'Come on, come on,' Scott whispered to himself as he tugged, his eyes eventually falling on a shiny new latch lock fitted further down. 'Oh, right.'

The muffled conversation from the room on his right stopped as he twisted the latch and pulled the door open. Scott was half in and half out of the house as the door to the kitchen opened. Matt and Darren stood in the doorway with their balaclavas rolled up on top of their heads like woolly hats and a surprised look on their faces at the sight of Scott exiting out of the front door. Scott took off across the gravel with Matt and Darren nearly falling out of the door after him. As Scott ran past the grey van with his eyes fixed on the woodland by the drive, Nick Temple stepped out from behind it and punched him with full force in the stomach. Scott's insides felt like they'd imploded. The air left his body and he crumpled to the floor desperately trying to breathe.

'How the fuck did he get out?' Temple yelled at the other two.

'Don't look at us. The first we knew about it, he was legging it out the front door,' Matt grumbled, grabbing Scott and dragging him off the floor.

'Fuck. Just get him inside and make sure he's tied up securely.'

While Matt took Scott back upstairs, Temple and Darren went through to the kitchen.

'It's alright, boss, he's back upstairs now, no harm done. You wanna brew?' Darren said, shaking the kettle at Temple.

'No, it's not alright, you dozy fucking pillock. He's seen our faces now, hasn't he?' Temple yelled, moving quickly over to Darren to pull the rolled up balaclava off the top of his head and throw it in his face. 'This changes everything and now I've got to phone Birchwood and explain what's happened.'

Temple stormed out the door, leaving Darren holding the kettle without answering him for fear of angering him further.

'Fuck me, he's got a face like a smacked arse,' Matt joked after seeing Temple head out the front door with his phone to his ear.

'Don't mate, he's fucking fuming.'

'Ah, he'll calm down. We got him, didn't we?' Matt said.

'Yeah, but he's seen our faces, hasn't he?'

'Shit,' Matt said, looking out the window to see Temple pacing the courtyard while talking on his phone.

In the upstairs bedroom, Scott sat in the chair coughing and wheezing, his eye swelling up where Matt had punched him in the face once he was back in the room. He tried to move, but Matt had wound the chain around his body and wrists and through the chair, fixing it with several padlocks so it held him tight to the back of the chair.

Well, that went well.

CHAPTER 40

Birchwood entered the Cabinet Office buildings in Whitehall for the second time in a week. Martin Webster met him as before and escorted him through security and off down the long corridor.

'Are they ready to sign?' Birchwood said in a hushed voice.

'I haven't had direct confirmation, but the meeting was put together within thirty minutes of the Heathrow attack, so all the signs are good.'

Birchwood didn't answer, a flicker of a smile forming on his face at the thought, changing back to his business-like poker face as he entered the COBR meeting room.

'Ah, Mr Birchwood, thank you for coming at such short notice. Please sit, sit.'

'You're welcome, Prime Minister, I'm happy to be of assistance,' Birchwood said looking around all the faces in the room, all familiar apart from a gentleman in an immaculate navy blue suit sitting to the right of the Prime Minister, his chair placed slightly away from the table at a sideways angle. The man sat with his legs crossed, his hands sitting comfortably in his lap as he looked intensely in Birchwood and Webster's direction.

'Prime Minister, may I ask why our Director of International Security is present in the meeting?' Webster said while looking at Simon like he was something he'd just stepped in.

'As Director of International and National Security, Simon has a vested interest in the implications of Project Spearhead and what it means for the security of the country. Now, if I may continue,' the PM said, his direct tone keeping Webster from protesting further.

'Yes, of course, sorry, Prime Minister. Please continue,' Webster said, backing down.

'Good. Mr Birchwood, the council is in full agreement, Project Spearhead has the green light, and after yesterday's attack on Heathrow Airport we can not express how urgently we need this system up and running,' the Prime Minister said, giving the nod to one of the Cabinet members who placed a folder with the signed official contract for Project Spearhead to go ahead.

'Thank you, Prime Minister, members of the council. Once I receive the seventy-five million initial payment as set out in page five of my proposal, I can bring in the teams to implement the system immediately,' said Birchwood, looking at the documents while hiding the buzz of excitement from his plans all coming to fruition inside.

The meeting went on for another twenty minutes while Birchwood answered questions about the implementation schedule of Project Spearhead. All the time, he was acutely aware of Simon watching without saying a word.

'Thank you, gentlemen, I think that concludes everything for today. Mr Webster, if you wouldn't mind reporting back to me once you have escorted Mr Birchwood out of the building. I need a full progress update on the investigation into Genesis UK.'

'Yes, Prime Minister, of course,' Webster said, unnerved by Simon leaning over to say something quietly to the Prime Minister while still looking in his direction. The two of them remained seated while everyone else filed out of the room.

Birchwood and Webster walked down the long corridor in silence, only speaking once they'd cleared security and stood outside the building by themselves.

'Well done, Alfred, you've done it.'

'Thank you, Martin, but don't get overexcited, we still have one final thing to do,' Birchwood said, looking around to make sure no one was in earshot.

'Don't worry, old man, I have the SCO19 team ready to go.'

'You trust them?'

'Totally, they're all handpicked men. I've briefed them on what to do,' Webster said, looking at his watch, eager not to keep the PM waiting too long.

'There's been a slight change to the plan.'

'What? Why didn't you say? No, this is too risky,' Webster said, panicking.

'I'm saying it now, Martin. Scott Miller got out and saw Nick and his men, which means he can identify them and that would lead back to me, which will lead back to you. Instead of rescuing him from the Genesis UK terrorists, the headline will have to read, *"Armed terrorists killed during hostage rescue attempt, police storm a farmhouse only to find Genesis UK had already killed Scott Miller."* Ok. The uniform, weapons and explosives from the Nova South attack will be in the farmhouse, along with a laptop containing evidence of their cyber attacks. Take care of everyone and get your team to use the weapon from the Nova South attack on Miller and its case closed. You'll be the PM's golden boy, and I'll stop you from going bankrupt by taking care of your bad business debts. Everybody wins.' Birchwood finished by patting Webster on the back.

'Ok, ok, I'd better go, we'll talk later,' Webster said reluctantly. His fear of bankruptcy, public humiliation, and prison outweighed his moral standing on murdering four innocent people.

He looked at his watch again and turned to head back to the building. As Birchwood turned with him, Simon walked out and looked their way. A small smile formed on his face as he nodded his acknowledgement of them before getting into the back of a car. The driver shut the door after, got in himself and pulled away into London's slow moving traffic.

'I don't like that guy. He gives me the creeps,' Webster said.

'Is he going to be a problem?' Birchwood replied.

'No, I've got full control over the Genesis UK investigation. He isn't a problem.'

'Good,' Birchwood said, leaving Webster to scoot back into the building.

Birchwood watched Simon's car moving slowly away in a line of traffic until it disappeared out of sight. He looked at the signed contracts in his hand before leaving the Cabinet Office buildings in Whitehall for the nearest Tube station.

CHAPTER 41

'**G**ood meeting, sir?' Simon's driver said over his shoulder.

'It was very interesting, Leonard. Oh, excuse me, I must get this,' Simon said, looking at the caller ID on his phone.

'Very good, sir,' Leonard replied. Paid for his discretion, he focused on his driving with no interest in any dealings Simon might be discussing on his phone.

'Edward.'

'I've got the remaining list of vans that can't be accounted for at the time of Scott's disappearance.'

'Excellent work, Edward. How many are we looking at?'

'Just six. I'll forward you the list of registered keepers now.'

'Thank you, Edward, and nobody at Special Branch knows we've been searching the ANPR cameras and DVLA database for the information?'

'No, I used a contact from inside. There's no MI6 information request and no paper trail,' Edward Jenkins replied.

'Good, leave it with me. I'll let you know how it pans out.'

'I take it our mutual friend is conducting the investigation?' Edward asked, even though he was sure he knew the answer.

'Do you know anyone better?' Simon answered bluntly.

'No, if anyone can find Scott and Genesis UK, Danny can. Good luck.'

'Thank you, Edward,' Simon said, hanging up.

His phone beeped a second later with the incoming information from Edward. Simon opened it and turned his phone sideways to get a better look as he scrolled through its contents. He skimmed through the details until he reached the bottom, frowning before scrolling back up to something that had caught his eye about the registered keeper for the third and fourth vehicles on the list.

2022 Ford Transit Van 2.0TDCI, colour Grey Matter, registered keeper: Birchwood McMillan Security Ltd.

'Mmm, I wonder,' Simon muttered to himself.

Flicking through his phone, Simon opened up a browser window and entered a Companies House search for Birchwood McMillan Security Ltd, a smile crossing his face when he saw that one of the company's directors was Alfred Birchwood.

'Interesting, and who are you?' he said, thinking out loud as he read the second named director, Donald McMillan.

A quick Google search told him that Donald McMillan had been a major investor in four of Alfred Birchwood's companies until he and his wife disappeared whilst on holiday in Mexico in July 2020. The authorities found blood in his hotel room, but no bodies were ever found. Donald McMillan was removed as a director from Companies House after the courts granted Alfred Birchwood sole directorship with McMillan missing, presumed dead.

'How very convenient.'

Simon copied the information and forwarded it to Danny's phone, along with Edward's file.

Please find attached vehicle registration information. You might want to start with the third and fourth vehicles on the list.

He noted the tick to say Danny had received his message but didn't get any reply.

'You've never been one for much conversation have you, Daniel?' he muttered.

'Pardon, sir?' said his driver from the front.

'Oh nothing, Leonard, just thinking out loud. Actually, change of plan, I'll be working from home for the rest of today. Drop me there and take the rest of the day off. I'll call you when I need you.'

'Very good, sir,' Leonard said, indicating before turning away from his original destination to head for Simon's home in St John's Wood.

CHAPTER 42

Danny sat in a Starbucks on the outskirts of Cambridge. He'd managed to convince Nikki that he should go alone as he'd probably spend the day chasing dead ends. With Scott's clients voicing their concern over missed appointments, Nikki reluctantly agreed so she could deal with the backlog of work. He was on his second cup of coffee when he received the message from Simon. He read the part saying to start with the third and fourth on the list, then opened the attachment and read the information on the registered keeper. Draining his coffee cup, Danny walked out of Starbucks and got back into his car, scrolling through his phone before calling an old friend.

'Greenwood International Security,' came a pleasant female voice.

'Paul Greenwood please.'

'I'm sorry, Mr Greenwood is in a meeting. Can I take a message?'

'Interrupt him. Tell him it's Danny Pearson and that Scott's in trouble.'

'But —'

'It'll be fine, I promise. Just do it please,' Danny said forcefully.

The line went quiet and for a little while.

'Daniel, it's Paul. What's happened to Scott? What do you need?' came Paul's welcome voice.

'Hi mate, Scott's been kidnapped by members of Genesis UK. I'm chasing leads but I need some background on a company. What do you know about Birchwood McMillan Security Ltd?'

'Birchwood McMillan, er, well, they're not really a security company in the sense that we are. They're an in-house corporate security firm, formed to provide security for the companies owned by their director, the technology giant Alfred Birchwood. The company's head of security is a guy called Nicholas Temple, a bit of an arsehole from what I remember. Rumour has it he was thrown out of the Parachute Regiment for gross misconduct. Why the interest?' Paul said, his curiosity piqued.

'They own a fleet of grey Ford Transit vans,' Danny said dryly.

'What? Grey Ford Transit vans? What's that got to do with anything?'

'Maybe nothing, but Scott was grabbed just before his meeting with the murdered head of the NCSC, Giles Wright, and whoever took him used a grey Ford Transit van with false plates. It disappeared somewhere in the Cambridge area, and Simon's narrowed it down to six vans registered in the Cambridge area.'

'And one of those vehicles belongs to Birchwood McMillan Security?'

'No, two of the vehicles belong to Birchwood McMillan Security. Hell of a coincidence, right?' Danny said, starting the car.

'Mmm, yes, and you know how I feel about coincidences.'

'Yep, never trust a coincidence. Thanks Paul,' Danny said,

thinking back to what Paul always said when he first knew him as an army intelligence officer.

'No problem. Let me know if you need anything else.'

'I will. See you, buddy.'

Danny hung up and reversed out of his parking place and headed off in the direction of Birchwood McMillan Security's registered offices. Following his sat nav, he turned into an industrial estate and drove slowly past plumbing and electrical wholesalers, a metal fabricating company and a double glazing firm before spotting the Birchwood McMillan Security's offices, which turned out to be nothing more than a large commercial unit with offices on the first floor. Pulling up a little way back from the building, Danny looked over at the vehicles parked in the spaces out front. A couple of cars, not expensive. Family cars, probably office staff. A grey Ford Transit van, but it was the wrong model and didn't have a registration plate that matched either of the ones on Simon's list. With no better options, Danny settled back in his seat and Googled the company's website on his phone for something to do while he staked out the offices. When he'd finished, Danny sent a message to Simon.

Get me all you have on Birchwood McMillan's head of security, Nicholas Temple.

Simon's reply came immediately back.

Give me twenty minutes.

While Danny waited, a grey Ford Transit van drove past him and turned into the car park outside Birchwood McMillan Security. Its registration plate matching the one on his list. A young man barely old enough to drive hopped out, dressed in greasy overalls with Henley Autos written on the back. He reached back into the van to remove a plastic disposable seat cover off the driver's seat, screwing it up before grabbing some paperwork off the dash. He locked the van and went inside the building. As he disappeared out of sight, a smaller van branded with Henley Autos drove past Danny and parked on the road in front of the offices. The driver wound the window down and sat with the engine running. Danny got out and walked over to him.

'Is it alright now?' he said to the driver, pointing to the van.

'Yeah, it was an intermittent sensor fault causing the engine management light to come on. Bastard to find though,' he said, happy to talk as he took Danny for someone that worked there.

'Must have been, you've had it a few days, haven't you?' Danny said casually as he edged towards the offices like he was heading in.

'No, longer than that. We picked it up at the beginning of last week. Should be fine now,' the guy said, looking around Danny at his apprentice coming out of the offices towards him.

'Ok, well thanks, mate,' Danny said, moving away from the van as if he was going towards the offices.

As soon as the apprentice got in the van, the mechanic turned it around and drove off like he was late for something. Danny spun on his heels and walked back to his car. As he crossed the van off his list, his phone pinged with an incoming message from Simon.

Temple's file attached.

Settling back into the driver's seat Danny read the file on Nicholas Temple. Apart from being court marshalled out of the Parachute Regiment for breaking his commanding officer's nose, and an old arrest sheet for actual bodily harm - case dropped - Temple had a clean sheet. There was nothing that would lead you to believe that kidnapping was part of his repertoire.

The afternoon ticked on with no sign of the remaining van on the list. Between four and five o'clock, the workers started leaving the building until the last one drove away. There had still been no sign of Temple. Danny looked at the address on the file from Simon and started the car before heading towards Temple's house.

Alarm bells rang the moment Danny pulled into the small estate with twenty or so five- and six-bedroom detached houses. The sun was getting low in the sky by the time he parked up twenty metres short of Temple's house. It was the largest on the estate and should be well outside the salary from a head of security position. A Porsche 718 Cayman GT4 RS worth over a hundred grand sitting on the drive only emphasised the point further. The sun slowly dipped behind the house, leaving it in darkness. Danny settled in his seat to play the waiting game once more.

'Hello love,' he said after his phone rang with Nikki's caller ID.

'How are you getting on? Is there any news on Scott?' she asked, trying to hide the worry in her voice.

'I think I'm getting closer. I've got a good lead on the van that took him,' Danny said, trying to sound positive.

'Good, are you coming home?' Nikki asked.

'No, I can't, not until I've found the van and Scott.'

'Ok, call me as soon as you have any news.'

'I will, and Nikki?'

'Yes?' she replied, her voice cracking, so he knew she was crying.

'I'll get him back, I promise.'

'I love you,' she said after a small pause.

'I love you too,' Danny replied, reluctantly hanging up.

He sat in darkness for a few hours, slapping his face and winding down the window now and then to take deep breaths of cool night air to keep himself awake. Around eleven o'clock, distant headlights illuminated the road behind him. Danny slid down in his seat as Nicholas Temple drove past in the grey van with the missing registration plate from Danny's list. He swung the van onto his drive and parked next to the Porsche. Temple got out of the van and went inside, the house lights coming on just after he closed the door. Danny sat up, weighing up his options. He could go in and shove a gun in Temple's face. But despite wanting answers and a release for his pent-up frustration, he didn't have a shred of proof that Temple was involved in Scott's abduction. Pushing his impatience down deep, Danny decided the best course of action was to follow the van when Temple left the house again. If it was involved in Scott's abduction, there was a high chance Temple would use it to return to wherever they were holding him.

He watched the shadowy outline of Temple inside the house, visible for only a second before he closed the blinds, shutting him out. Danny started to feel exposed sitting in his parked car in an expensive estate, the kind of estate where people would notice a stranger in a car, an estate where people would ring the police if they saw someone sitting watching a house all night. He started the engine and drove slowly away. There was only one road in and out of the estate, so he didn't need to sit directly outside Temple's house. He exited the estate onto the main road and took the first left into a less desirable 1960s built estate. After spinning the car around, Danny drove back to the main road, parking the car just short of the junction. He turned the engine off and relaxed into the driving seat, preparing himself for a long night of watching the exit to Temple's estate around twenty five metres away.

CHAPTER 43

The heat hit Silus Montague as he exited Bangkok's Suvarnabhumi Airport, with sweat patches appearing under his armpits. He put his luggage in the boot and climbed into a taxi. Sitting back, he relaxed on the long drive to his newly rented apartment in Pattaya City. Unzipping his bag, he looked again at his new passport, driving licence, and birth certificate supplied by Alfred Birchwood. He smiled and zipped them back inside his bag. Taking the brand new phone from his pocket, he logged into the bank account set up under his new identity. The recently credited two million pounds from a shell company that banked in The Bahamas looked back at him. For the first time in years, Silus, or as he was now known by his new identity, Kenneth Wilson, relaxed.

The sun had gone down by the time he tipped the driver who dropped him at the apartment Birchwood had arranged for him. He climbed the stairs to find a teenage boy waiting for him at the top, a brown Jiffy bag in his hand.

'Mr Wilson?' he said in heavily accented English.

'Er, yes,' Montague replied, the name feeling alien to him.

'Here, it's the keys to your apartment,' the boy said, handing the Jiffy bag over with a skinny arm.

Montague reached out, sliding his hand over the boy's hand to curl his finger around the boy's wrist, the hold lingering a second or two longer than it should have.

'Thank you,' Montague said, releasing his grip to pluck the bag from the boy's hand.

The teenager smiled, pulling away slowly before moving around Montague to disappear down the stairs, Montague's eyes following him as he went.

I think I'm going to like it here.

He unlocked the door and went inside. The apartment was neat and tidy and not too big in size. It would do him well until he found the right place to buy. He opened up the shutters and looked down on the busy street below, lit up by the bright neon signs from the shops and bars lining each side. He spotted the teenage boy standing on the opposite side of the road, talking with some of his friends. As Montague looked them up and down, the teenager turned his head and looked up at him, an innocent smile on his face. His lithe teenage body stirred parts of Montague's body he'd been repressing for a long time.

Picking out a shirt and cotton trousers, he decided to leave the rest of the unpacking until later and headed into the bathroom to freshen up. Ten minutes later he walked down the stairs and onto the street, feeling a pang of disappointment that the teenager was no longer in sight. Shaking it off, Montague headed in the direction of Pattaya's infamous Boyz Town, with its bars and clubs and young men willing to accommodate an array of fantasies for a price. Montague quickened his step, eager to explore this new land of opportunities. He walked under the neon Boyz Town sign spanning the road, announcing the start of the gay red-light district.

Montague ignored the advances of tight T-shirt-wearing young Thai men touting for business. They were cute but he had something younger in mind. He meandered along, taking in the sights, stopping in his tracks when he spotted the teenage boy from the apartment sitting at a table outside a bar nearby. The boy looked his way and smiled sweetly. Full of confidence, Montague felt reborn, free of his past life, a new country, a new identity and a fortune in the bank. Montague walked over to the boy.

'Mr Wilson, it's nice to see you again,' the boy said, smiling, his eyes looking innocently up at Montague.

'And it's nice to see you, too. Would you like a drink?' Montague said, letting his hand rest on the boy's thigh for a few seconds.

'I'll have a beer,' the boy replied, sliding his hand on top of Montague's, stopping him from moving it away.

They chatted for a while, the boy getting closer to him all the time. Montague lapped up the attention, tilting his head when the boy leaned in and whispered, 'Do you want to go somewhere quiet, just the two of us?'

Montague nodded, letting the boy take his hand and lead him away from the bar. Consumed with his desire to have the boy, Montague didn't see the two men get up from a table close by to follow a few paces behind them.

'It's not far. Come this way,' the boy said, leading Montague away from the bright lights into the dark back streets. 'Just down here.'

The boy took him down a narrow alley, both of them turning to outlined shadows as the streetlight behind them struggled to penetrate the narrow gap between the buildings. A shadowy figure stepped into the alley ahead of them. The boy suddenly left Montague and scooted past the figure, snatching the wad of notes from his outstretched hand before disappearing into the darkness. Montague backed up, a cold sweat washing over him. He turned to head back towards the street, only to see another shadowy figure heading his way, the glint of a knife visible in his hand.

'Look, I have money, take it. Here, take it. Just let me go, it's yours.'

Featureless in the dark, the figure kept approaching, while the footsteps of his accomplice grew louder behind Montague's. With fear running through his body, Montague pulled off his watch and held it up with his wallet, offering them in the hope they would leave him alone.

A whisper from behind him sent Montague's mind spinning.

'Mr Birchwood sends his regards.'

Before he could react, the two men stabbed Montague repeatedly from in front and behind. Montague stood upright, rooted to the spot, paralysed in fear and shock, unable to process what was happening as they punched the blades into his body. The brain's self-preservation mechanism shielded him from pain and panic until the body could take no more and he slumped to the floor. He felt the two men rifling through his pockets before picking up the wallet and watch and disappearing into the darkness. As he bled out onto the cold alley floor, Montague's world faded away.

Across the city, two men packed up his things and cleared them out of the apartment. Six thousand miles away, Alfred Birchwood received the message that Montague was no more. He smiled to himself and returned to his computer, signing into Montague's bank account before transferring the two million pounds into an untraceable offshore bank account.

CHAPTER 44

Temple noticed the car parked near his house. He also caught a glimpse of the shadowy figure sitting in the driver's seat. He didn't look over when he stepped out of the van, opting to enter the house and look out from behind the cover of darkness within the house. It was too dark to see the driver, so he turned on the lights and shut the blinds. By the time he'd moved into the dining room to take another look, the car had gone and he put it down to paranoia, shutting the blinds before moving out of the room. His phone buzzed with a message from Birchwood.

It's on for tomorrow. Clean up and be out by 9am.

Without replying, Temple selected a contact and hit dial.
'Boss,' came Matt's answer.
'How's our guest?'
'Still whingeing. Darren checked on him earlier. He's ok.'
'Good, listen, they're going in tomorrow morning. You and Darren clean up and bag up everything you've used. I'll be there at eight with the gear from London. We'll put it in place and fuck off before it goes down.'

'Thank Christ for that. If I have to look after that wanker upstairs for one minute longer, I'll do him myself.'

'Just clean the place up properly. Use the chemical cleaner I left you, ok? I don't want anything coming back on us,' Temple growled, pausing before adding, 'Do I make myself clear, Matt?' to emphasise the point. He was in no mood for Matt's jokes.

'Yes boss, crystal. We'll be ready.' Matt replied, dropping the jovial tone.

'Make sure you are,' Temple added before hanging up.

Moving into his office, Temple looked at the checkerboard display from his security cameras on a monitor fixed to the wall. There was no sign of the car so he moved to his desk and turned the computer on. With too much going on in his head to relax, Temple answered some emails and ran through work schedules and paperwork. When he'd finished, he turned the computer off and sat back in his chair.

Just one more day and this whole Genesis UK thing will be over. All the loose ends will be tied up. Birchwood got his contract and I'll get my payout.

CHAPTER 45

'Evening, Jarvis, has my guest arrived?' Simon said as the concierge of the Britannia Gentlemen's Club took his coat on arrival.

'Good evening, sir. Yes, I've shown him to your usual table in the Henry VIII lounge. Would you like me to put your briefcase in one of the secure lockers?'

'No thank you, Jarvis, I'll keep it with me. I'll have my usual, if I may.'

'Of course, sir, I'll bring it to your table,' Jarvis said, gesturing for Simon to go on ahead of him to his table.

Simon smiled back before walking through the club to the small oak panelled lounge at the rear of the building, its intimate booths used by politicians and businessmen over decades for discussions and decisions that had shaped the country.

'Evening, Hank, good of you to come. I see Jarvis is taking care of you,' Simon said, shaking Hank's hand after he put his scotch on the rocks down.

'My pleasure. I have to confess that when the head of Department D requested an informal chat, my curiosity was piqued,' replied Hank Samson, Senior CIA representative for the UK, tipping his drink to Simon before taking a sip.

Simon smiled and sat quietly as Jarvis approached with his vodka and tonic. 'Thank you, Jarvis, that will be all for now,' he said, pausing the conversation again until Jarvis had moved out of earshot before continuing.

'Now, now, Hank, you know very well there is no Department D,' Simon added, the both of them sharing a knowing look.

'Of course, and your name's not really Simon, and I assume we were never here,' Hank said with a smile.

'Shall I continue?' Simon said, ignoring the last comment.

'Please do.'

'I'm sure you're aware of our current difficulties with the group calling themselves Genesis UK.'

'I am. Terrible business,' Hank said, wondering where the conversation was going.

'Well, it would appear that the bombing of the Red Lion public house and the assassination of Giles Wright, the CEO of the NCSC, not to mention half a dozen members of the security services, is down to one of yours,' Simon said, his manner still pleasant and upbeat as he placed his briefcase on his lap and opened it. He fetched a file from within and handed it to Hank.

'An American?'

'A former Navy Seal no less. A very highly skilled individual, possibly more than just a Navy Seal,' Simon said as Hank opened the file and flicked through the contents.

Simon sipped his drink patiently, studying Hank's reaction as he looked over the details of the pub bombing and the attack on the Nova South building. Hank's eyebrows raised slightly and his focus intensified as he studied Scott's enhanced AI reconstruction of Johnson's build and facial features.

'Care to share?' Simon said when Hank's eyes finally left the page to look at him.

'Unofficially?' Hank said quietly, his face losing all the softness of their earlier greeting.

'Of course, as you said, this meeting never happened,' Simon answered, taking a sip of his drink.

'His name was, or apparently still is, Oliver Johnson. He was one of our high-level assets. In fact, he was one of our best assets. He disappeared four years ago on a mission to take out an American millionaire who was funding a splinter group of Al Qaeda. It all went wrong, the millionaire never showed and Johnson was captured. They sent the usual propaganda video - Johnson tied up in a basement, three masked men standing behind him armed with a machete. Naturally, we assumed they'd killed him and left his body to rot in the desert.'

'No black ops team charging to the rescue then?'

'Come on, Simon, you know better than that. He was an asset in a foreign land on a mission that officially never happened.'

'Mmm, yes, quite. The only problem now is what do we do with him? He's committed some very public and nasty attacks on English soil, and that has got the politicians baying for blood. Not to mention he killed several Secret Service agents, some of which were mine, and that doesn't sit well with me. The government needs to stamp out Genesis UK and bring someone to justice, and they need to do it quickly if they are to restore public confidence in its democratically elected party. However, it will cause a media shitstorm if it becomes public knowledge that a rogue CIA asset murdered the CEO of the NCSC and blew up three British politicians in the Red Lion bombing,' Simon said, his voice calm and friendly as he chose his words very carefully.

'You have a suggestion?' Hank said, expecting some sort

of compromise that may involve favours owed or information shared.

Simon gave Hank a smile, then gave a small wave to a waitress on the other side of the room.

'Another drink,' Simon said smugly, knowing he had the upper hand in the discussion.

CHAPTER 46

Danny had watched the sun come up and had some funny looks from an early morning dog walker as he hung his head out of the open car window to wake himself up. He ate half a Mars bar he found in the glove box and listened to the eight o'clock news on the radio. Cracking the stiffness out of his neck, Danny yawned and stretched, then rubbed his eyes. He was about to give Nikki a call when Temple rolled the grey van to a stop at the turning out of his estate. Instantly awake, Danny started the engine while watching Temple indicate and turn on to the main road to head away from him. Danny let a couple of cars pass before he turning and following at a safe distance. They flowed with the traffic for a couple of miles and entered the village of Sarston. At the end of the village, Temple took a right turn and headed out into the countryside. Danny turned and pulled back, tailing the van by the intermittent sight of the roof section above the winding hedge lined country lane.

The distance closed a bit as the van slowed and turned, disappearing into trees on Danny's left. When Danny reached the spot where the van had turned, he read the sign for Pinewood Farm screwed to the front of an open five bar wooden gate. Swinging his head to the side, he caught a glimpse of the van as it disappeared into the woods on the long drive leading to the farmhouse. Continuing down the lane at a crawl, Danny spotted an opening on the opposite side of the road leading into a farmer's field. He stopped level with the gap and checked if the field was level enough for him to park on. Seeing that it was, he bumped up through the gap and parked the car out of sight behind the hedge. Opening the glove box, he grabbed his gun, immediately wishing he hadn't put his holdall containing the rifle and gun back under the base of the wardrobe when they returned from the fixers. Tucking the gun into the back of his jeans, Danny ran back up the road to the five bar gate and the entrance to the long gravel drive through the woods. He took a last look up and down the road, then pulled the gun from his jeans and jogged up the drive after the van. As he rounded the bend, he ducked into the woods when he got a glimpse of the farmhouse a hundred metres ahead of him.

With the view lost behind the dense pine trees, Danny pushed on through the branches until he could see the court-yard, the van and farmhouse from behind the final row of trees. Temple was dragging a medium-sized black suitcase from the back of the van. He was having a conversation with a man standing in the farmhouse doorway, dressed in a navy blue boiler suit, latex gloves and a woolly hat pulled tightly on top of his head. Danny could tell the suitcase was heavy by the way Temple moved it. The man in the doorway disappeared inside and Temple followed close behind with the suitcase. A couple of minutes later, Danny watched a third man, also dressed in a boiler suit, hat and gloves, carry bin bags out of the farmhouse, chucking them into the back of the van before returning inside.

Pushing a branch to one side, Danny took in his surroundings. There was a fenced in overgrown meadow with wood-land beyond on one side, and a large open hay barn on the other side. Other than old tractors and various plough attachments and farming machinery, the barn was the same as the meadow, old and neglected. With no other vehicles in sight, Danny hoped that the two men and Temple were the only ones in the house. Resisting the urge to storm the house, he crouched back down, opting to watch for a little bit longer to make sure he knew what he was up against. After all, he didn't even know if Scott was in there.

CHAPTER 47

Temple dumped the suitcase down onto the dining table and unzipped it. He folded the lid back and reached inside with his latex gloved hands, lifting the counter terrorism officer's uniform out to place it on the table beside a laptop full of incriminating information about Genesis UK that Birchwood had given him. After placing the helmet on top of the uniform, he took out the handgun and rifle and laid them out before placing the bomb making timers, explosives and detonators next to the other items.

'Is it clean?' Temple said, shutting the empty case and zipping it back up before placing it on the floor.

'Yeah,' said Matt casually as he walked out of the kitchen.

'Don't fuck me about, Matt. Is it clean and I mean really clean, fucking spotless,' Temple said, raising his voice.

'Yes, Nick, it's fucking clean, ok?' Matt answered, pissed off at being challenged.

'Good, where's Darren?'

'He's washing the downstairs bog down with bleach.'

'Ok, good. You take the suitcase, put it in the van and wait outside. Don't come back into the house and don't touch anything. I'm going to unchain Miller, then we're out of here,'

Temple said, checking his watch to make sure they were good for time.

Temple waited until Matt left the room then went into the kitchen and stood in the middle. He did a slow three-sixty check to make sure Matt had cleaned the place up properly. Satisfied, he moved back out into the hall just as Darren appeared carrying a bin bag with all the cleaning stuff from scrubbing the toilet.

'You got everything, right?' Temple said, frowning.

'Yes boss, you could eat your dinner off that crapper,' Darren said, grinning.

'Good, put the bag in the van and wait out there with Matt. I'll only be a minute.'

While Darren headed out the front door, Temple moved up the stairs, keeping to the middle so he didn't touch the bannisters, even though he had latex gloves on. He stopped outside the bedroom door to roll the woolly hat into a balaclava even though Scott had already seen his face, then turned the key in the lock and entered the room. Scott sat in the chair looking back at Temple defiantly, the chain still firmly fixed around his torso and through the chair. He flinched when Temple approached him, leaning in close to his face.

'Listen very carefully. I'm going to unchain you now. When I do, you stay in this room and sit tight. Someone is on their way to pick you up and take you home.'

Scott stared at the eyes looking back at him through the balaclava. 'You're letting me go, but I've seen your faces?'

Temple ignored the comment and finished unlocking the padlock then removed the chain, coiling it up while backing away towards the door.

'Just do as you're told, wait there and everything will be alright,' Temple said, backing out the door and closing it behind him without locking it.

He headed back downstairs without touching anything

then walked out of the front door, stopping to turn after a couple of paces, pulling his balaclava off as he looked at the farmhouse.

'Did you clean the front door?' he said, turning to look at Matt and Darren.

'Yeah, I did. Even used the stuff you gave me, just like you told me to,' Matt grumbled.

Temple took a last look at the open door then walked to the van.

'Get in,' he said, throwing the chain in the back of the van and sliding the door shut before climbing into the driving seat.

Taking a final look at the farmhouse and then at his watch, Temple started the van and spun it around on the gravel before driving off down the long drive.

CHAPTER 48

anny watched the van go. He'd seen them load the van with bags, he'd seen the latex gloves, and seen Temple coming out of the house with the balaclava on. It was obvious they were cleaning up whatever had been going on in the farmhouse. He just hoped that didn't include killing Scott. He gave the van a minute or so to reach the country lane at the end of the gravel drive, then pushed himself out from behind the trees. With his gun up, he ran across the courtyard, his head and gun moving in sync as he looked from window to window, to the open farmhouse door, searching for any sign of movement from within the house. When none presented itself, he flattened himself against the brickwork on one side of the open front door.

After a quick count of three to compose himself, Danny swung through into the hall. He moved in an arch, listening to the sounds of the house as looked from the door on his right, then up the stairs to the landing, ending on the door to his left. There was no one in sight, and no obvious sounds of anyone moving about. He moved into the dining room, noticing the items from the Nova South attack spread out on the table as he continued into the kitchen. When he found no one there, he relaxed a little and moved back to the dining room. Lowering his gun, Danny picked up the helmet that went with the counter terrorism officer's uniform. The sound of a floorboard creaking overhead made him freeze. With his eyes raised to the ceiling, Danny carefully placed the helmet back down and picked his gun up. He left the room and headed up the stairs, treading lightly on the edge of the steps closest to the wall, where it was less likely to creak and announce his approach.

With his body behind the cover of the landing wall, Danny reached towards the bedroom doorknob, preparing to spin around and fire into the bedroom after he pushed it open. To his surprise, the door opened before he got his hand to it. Instinct and training took over, Danny flicked his eyes down the sights of his raised gun, his finger tensing on the hair trigger. Scott's eyes went wide as he peered onto the landing to find the barrel of a gun millimetres away from his face, his features only relaxing when his eyes worked their way back along the arm to see Danny's set-in-stone face looking back at him.

'Good lord, do you have to do that? I nearly had a heart attack,' Scott said with a sigh of relief.

'Nice to see you too, Scotty boy,' Danny said, dropping the gun to look into the bedroom.

'Yes, quite. Well, I'm glad they sent you to pick me up. Shall we go?' Scott said, walking casually past Danny.

'What do you mean, sent me? No one sent me,' Danny replied, turning to follow Scott.

'The bad guys, they untied me and said someone was coming to pick me up.'

The hairs on Danny's neck stood up. The empty farmhouse, the stuff from the Nova South attack and Scott roaming around freely. None of it added up, and that gave him a really bad feeling about being there.

'We should go. Now, Scott,' he said, overtaking him to the top of the stairs.

'What, oh, right you are then.'

They got halfway down the stairs when a young woman with green hair and dark eyeliner walked in through the open front door. A tall, skinny guy with long hair and a patchy beard followed close behind her. There was a third person, but he was barely visible behind the tall guy. Danny had his gun trained on them in the blink of an eye, puzzled by their looks and apparent lack of weapons.

'Whoa, take it easy, it's us, Genesis UK,' Sebastian said, excitedly pointing to himself and the other two. 'You're the guy, right? The one who's been helping us,' Sebastian continued, still standing in the doorway as Rachael and Tobias moved inside to stand beside him.

'Tell me exactly why you are here. Now,' Danny growled, his gun still pointing at Sebastian's forehead as he moved down the stairs with Scott following closely behind him.

'Ok, ok, shit, don't shoot,' Sebastian said, putting his hands up. 'We were told to come here to meet the man who's been funding us. The government guy who believes in our cause, he's been helping us to fight for a better future. When he and his followers overthrow the government, Genesis UK will rise up and—'

'Shut the fuck up, dipshit,' interrupted Danny, looking to the side of Sebastian through the open door at movement in the tree line on the other side of the courtyard. 'Get away from the door.'

Danny's cry was too late. A double-tap of rifle fire sounded off and two bullets simultaneously ripped through the front of Sebastian's chest, killing him instantly. He dropped to the floor with a look of shocked surprise locked on his face. Danny swiftly barged Rachael away from the open door, kicking it shut as she screamed in horror at Sebastian's body.

As the latch clicked shut on the slamming door, two more bullets blasted through the wood, throwing a shower of splinters across the stone floor before lodging into the staircase.

'Everyone keep down and follow me,' Danny shouted, looking towards the dining room, only to see Rachael standing in front of the little square window to one side of the hall. 'Get away from the window.'

His words were lost on her. She was in shock and frozen with fear. Before he could push her to one side, a bullet popped through the glass and entered the back of her head. When it exited the other side, it ripped most of her face off in a plume of red mist that hung in the air for a second or two after her body had flopped to the floor.

'Go, go,' Danny said, grabbing Tobias by the arm and pulling him into the dining room while pushing Scott in front of him.

'What the hell is going on?' Scott said, crouching with his back against the wall.

'It's a setup. They're cleaning house,' Danny answered, checking and loading the handgun on the table. 'Scott, take this, just point and squeeze, ok, and try not to blow your bollocks off.'

'Got it,' Scott said, taking it from Danny's hand.

'You, what's your name?' Danny said, locking eyes with Tobias, who was crying and shaking badly. 'Oi, look at me, son. What's your name?' Danny repeated in a louder voice, to get Tobias to focus on him.

'T-T-Tobias,' he stammered.

'Good. Listen, Tobias, I'm going to get us out of here, but I need you to do exactly as I say. Ok?'

Tobias wiped the snot from his nose and nodded to show he understood.

'Ok, let me just have a look at what's going on, then we're going to see if we can get out through the kitchen,' Danny said, leaving Scott and Tobias in the corner while he ducked down and moved to one side of the dining room window.

Darting his head across just far enough to see out, Danny took a mental snapshot of the courtyard, taking in the five-strong SCO19 police unit approaching the house in a well-practised formation.

Fuck, this shit just gets better by the minute.

'What is it?' Scott said, looking across at Danny.

'You don't want to know, mate,' Danny grumbled, spinning away from the window on his knees before hopping up onto his feet. 'Stay where you are,' he said, tucking his gun into the back of his jeans as he ran into the kitchen.

Come on, come on, I need to move faster.

Ripping through the kitchen cupboards, Danny grabbed an old mixing bowl before pulling the cutlery drawer out and dumping the contents into the bowl. He hurtled back into the dining room to the table. Putting the bowl on its surface, he grabbed one of the blocks of C4 explosive and thumped a detonator into it. Uncoiling the two attached wires, he bit into the plastic and pulled to strip the ends, twisting them around the terminals on a timer. He looked up, visualising the approaching team's movements, then set the timer for ninety seconds. Pushing the C4 down into the cutlery filled bowl, Danny ran back into the hall and stopped beside Sebastian's body. He reached over him and placed the bowl so it was in line with the front door. Spinning on his heels, Danny moved quickly into the dining room, shutting the door behind him.

'We need to move, guys. Now, go, go. Keep low and follow me,' Danny said, herding them into the kitchen.

CHAPTER 49

'**R**ed Leader to Command, preparing to enter the farmhouse.'

'Affirmative, Red Leader,' said the radio operator, sitting in the back of a command truck parked in the woods around a hundred metres from the farmhouse.

The operator next to him gently pushed a joystick to zoom the camera mounted on a drone in as it flew high above the courtyard. Standing behind them, Martin Webster watched the camera feed on the screen. The SCO19 team split just before the door to the farmhouse, two of them flattening themselves against the brickwork on the left-hand side, standing one behind the other with their rifles up. The other two members of the team mirrored them on the right-hand side, while a fifth man knelt down on the courtyard ten feet back, looking down his sights at the centre of the door, ready to fire if anyone came charging out.

'Red One to Red Five, initiate breach.'

'Affirmative, Red One,' the kneeling man replied, immediately giving two short bursts of fire at the centre of the door, ripping through the wood like a knife through butter.

The second he'd finished, the front man on the left moved

around and kicked the door open, stepped inside and ducking left to let his wingman move in behind him. Moving as one with their rifles, they covered the stairs and hall, their eyes searching through the dusty air for their targets.

'Hall's clear,' came over the radio, the words barely leaving his headset before the C4 detonated inside the mixing bowl, the blast fragmenting it into a thousand sharp ceramic shards followed by pieces of razor sharp torn up cutlery all travelling at high velocity inside a ball of superheated gasses.

The two officers were caught in the middle of the three hundred and sixty degree blast. Flying shrapnel embedded itself into their body armour, helmet and goggles, ripping through the grey overall material into the flesh of their arms and legs as the blast wave picked them up and threw them back out the door to land on the courtyard outside.

Back in the command vehicle, the two controllers and Webster yanked the headphones off their heads, the sound of the explosion deafening them. Shaking their heads, they quickly put the headphones back on and called the team.

'Command to Red Team, come in, Red Team.'

'Red One to Command, Red Three's dead. Red Four is conscious but has multiple lacerations and burns. His breathing is OK, and he has minimal blood loss.'

'What the fuck? There's only supposed to be three kids and the computer nerd here,' came the transmission from Red Two.

'Get a grip on yourself, see how Wayne's doing,' said Red One to the man beside him.

Red Five remained on one knee, covering the opening into the farmhouse through the gap around the door as it swung precariously on one hinge.

'Listen to me, Wayne, you're going to be alright, mate, I can't see any arterial bleeding, ok? Just hang in there,' Red Two said to Red Four.

'Armed hostile ten o'clock,' shouted Red Five, squeezing

off shots towards Danny as he sprinted from the kitchen on the side of the farmhouse to the hay barn thirty metres away from them.

'Who the hell is that?' said Martin Webster in the command vehicle, watching the drone image of Danny disappearing into the barn.

'Red One to Command. Me and Red Five are going after hostile. Red Two is proceeding into the farmhouse to look for suspects,' Red One said, signalling Red Five to move to the barn.

'Affirmative Red One, I'll try to get eyes on the hostile,' said the drone operator, dropping the drone down to ten feet off the deck to fly it through the open barn door.

Splitting wide, Red One and Red Five moved across either side of the courtyard, eyes looking down the sights of their rifles at the open hay barn door as the drone disappeared inside.

In the command truck, Webster bent over to get a closer look at the camera feed over the operator's shoulder. Once the drone was inside, the operator took it up high into the rafters, moving it slowly around until he located Danny amongst large pieces of farm machinery. He zoomed in as Danny looked up, alerted by the buzzing rotor blades. With a clear picture of Danny's face filling the screen in the command truck, he pointed his gun at the drone and squeezed the trigger, sending the screen in the command vehicle into black with the words *Lost Signal* written boldly across the centre. Webster stood back with a frown on his face. He'd seen that face before but couldn't quite place it.

'My god, I've got it. I've read his file. He's one of Simon's men. What the hell is he doing here?' Webster said, more to himself than anyone else.

That bastard Simon's been going behind my back.

Back at the farmhouse, Red One and Red Five folded themselves flat against the outside wall of the barn. Red One looked across at Red Five and nodded. The two of them moved one step at a time towards the opening. They stopped just short while Red One counted his fingers down to go.

Three, two, one.

On one they both pivoted around the entrance, their rifles and heads moving as one as they searched for signs of movement.

Webster opened the back door of the command vehicle and looked at four men standing around in full SCO19 kit. 'We've got an unexpected visitor at the farmhouse. Get over there fast. Red One and Red Five have him trapped in the barn. I want him dead. There's a ten grand bonus to the first one to kill him.'

The four men grinned and burst into action, heading off through the trees towards the farmhouse.

CHAPTER 50

'**A**nswer your fucking phone, Simon,' Danny muttered, moving around the back of the barn with the phone glued to his ear.

'Daniel,' came Simon's usual unemotional response.

'I've got Scott and what's left of Genesis UK,' Danny said, keeping his voice low while squatting down behind a large metal oil drum.

'I'm guessing that, by what's left of Genesis UK means there's a problem of some sort?'

'Yes, there's a fucking problem alright. I followed Temple to a farmhouse. When he and his men cleared out, I found Scott wandering about upstairs. We were just about to leave when three dumb-arsed kids turned up. The place is one big setup, the kit used at Nova South is here and so is an SCO19 team, and trust me, they aren't looking to make arrests. They executed two of the kids without announcing themselves. I could really do with some fucking help pretty fucking quickly, or you're not going to have anyone left to tell you who's really behind Genesis UK.'

'Where are you?'

'Pinewood Farm, it's about two miles outside of the village of Sarston, north of Cambridge.'

'I'll have someone with you as soon as I can,' Simon said, his voice still calm and matter of fact.

'Just make it sooner rather than later,' Danny said, wasting his breath. Simon had already hung up.

Danny looked over the top of the metal drum towards the entrance to the barn. Glancing down, he dipped his finger into a large drum full of a black liquid, realising it was engine oil as he rubbed it between his fingers. It had probably been sitting there for years, left over from oil changes in one or more of the old tractors. He looked out across the centre of the barn, then back at the drum before grabbing the metal rim with both hands. Pulling it with all his might, Danny managed to tilt the bottom of the heavy drum off the floor. He kept on pulling it until the oil slopped over the top and the drum sat balanced perfectly on its bottom rim. It passed the point of no return and gravity did the rest, pulling it crashing onto its side with a massive wave of oil rolling out across the smooth concrete floor of the barn. It continued to spread and thin out, covering most of the barn's centre as the two men from Red Team entered. Danny retreated out of sight amongst the farm machinery.

Lying on his side, Danny looked down the sights of his gun. There was a narrow view of the centre of the barn between the blades of a ploughing rig and under a tractor. The legs of Red One and Red Five came into view, their feet slipping on the oil as they tried to keep in formation while looking for Danny. Taking a breath then exhaling slowly, Danny squeezed off two rounds, ripping into Red One's heel through his boot with the first shot before cutting a clean hole through his calf muscle with the second shot. As Red One dropped screaming in agony onto the slippery oil covered floor, Red Five whipped his rifle around, blindly laying down covering fire in the general direction of the shots. Sliding out from under the ploughing rig, Danny fast-crawled around the back of the barn, keeping his head low as bullets ricocheted off the metal farm equipment around him.

'It's alright, I'll get you out of here,' Red Five yelled, his magazine running empty.

He ejected it and slammed in a new one from a pocket on his vest. Grabbing Red One by the back of his body armour, Red Five started dragging him backward towards the barn door, slipping and sliding on the oil, his rifle swinging around in his free hand as he looked for signs of Danny as he retreated.

While this was happening, Danny circled his way around to the opposite side of the barn. He watched from behind Red Five as he dragged his injured colleague towards the door.

Hopping up onto a flatbed trailer, Danny exploded into a run, diving off the far end to grab Red Five around the neck as he landed. The force sent them flying over the injured man to land heavily on the oil covered concrete floor.

Red Five's rifle clattered away under a tractor as they slid across the smooth concrete floor on a layer of engine oil. As they came to a stop, Danny jumped on Red Five's back and locked his arm around Red Five's throat in a choke hold, wrapping his legs around the man's body to stop him from getting free. The SCO19 officer thrashed around wildly, but Danny held on tight until the man's body went limp as he passed out. Danny kept the hold up for a few seconds longer to make sure he was fully unconscious, then released and kicked him off before rolling away.

Standing up covered in oil, Danny got to his feet and walked towards Red One who was trying to shuffle his way out of the barn. Panicking at Danny's approach, he scrabbled for the handgun in the holster on his side, his oil covered hands slipping on the catch to release it. Before he could get it out, Danny pulled the gun from the back of his jeans and pointed it at Red One's forehead. He stepped forward and placed his boot onto Red One's injured leg and pushed down. Screaming in pain, Red One put his palm up to Danny and begged him to stop.

Danny reached down and ripped the cable out from Red One's throat mic and earphones, cutting them off from the radio pack. 'Who are you working for?'

Trembling and in extreme pain, Red One gritted his teeth and said nothing, his eyes looking defiantly at Danny.

'I'm not fucking around here, pal, I'll count to three then you're gone,' Danny said, placing the barrel of his gun on the bridge of Red One's nose just under his helmet.

'One, two, three.'

'Ok, ok, Martin Webster, the Minister for Security. He's in a command vehicle parked in the woods.'

Danny lowered the gun and glanced out of the barn door while he contemplated his next move. He looked back down at Red One and bent down to take his gun, tucking it into the back of his jeans. He removed Red One's handcuffs and dragged him groaning in pain to the trailer, handcuffing his wrist through the metal struts of the towing rig. Leaving Red One, Danny slipped and slid over to Red Five, dragging him over to the trailer and handcuffing him next to Red One. Before leaving the barn, Danny removed Red Five's radio set and listened to the radio chatter as he walked out the door.

'Red One, Red Five, come in please. Red Two, what's your status?'

'Red Two, sweeping the farmhouse.'

'Affirmative, Red Two. We have lost radio contact with Red One and Red Five. Be advised that Blue Team has been dispatched, ETA four minutes.'

'Shit,' Danny grunted, heading for the farmhouse.

CHAPTER 51

Moving carefully into the dining room, Red Two twisted his head and rifle in unison to check out the corners of the room. Satisfied it was clear, he did a quick check behind him before moving cautiously towards the kitchen door.

'Red Two to Command, living room, hall and dining room are clear. I'm heading into the kitchen before doing a sweep of the upstairs rooms.'

While folded against the wall on one side of the kitchen door, Red Two pushed it open with the end of his rifle until it swung far enough to see in. The room looked empty so he moved inside. Treading softly, he moved around the kitchen island, darting his head and rifle across to check the gap on the far side. It was clear. A tapping noise startled him. His eyes flicked to the back door on the far side of the kitchen. It was slightly ajar, tapping the frame now and then as it swung gently in the breeze, the hay barn intermittently visible through the narrow opening.

'Red Two to Command, kitchen is clear, I'm heading upstairs,' he said, backing out of the room, preparing to head upstairs for a room sweep.

He turned in the kitchen doorway and had one foot in the dining room when a noise coming from behind the door to an old fashioned larder cupboard stopped him in his tracks.

Gotcha.

His mouth curled up into a smile. He stepped back into the kitchen and turned to face the larder door, his rifle pointing at its centre, the perfect height to hit centre body mass. The sound of a sneeze from inside the cupboard confirmed someone was inside. Red Two looked down the rifle sights, slowly increasing the pressure on the trigger until he'd reached the two pounds of pressure needed to move it. As the rifle teetered on the edge of firing, the barrel of a Glock handgun slid under the lip of Red Two's helmet, its muzzle pushing into his temple.

'I wouldn't do that if I were you. Now drop the rifle on the floor and put your hands behind your head, slowly, understand?' Danny said from behind him.

'Ok, ok, I understand,' Red Two answered, dropping the rifle with a metallic clatter on the stone floor.

Triggered by the sound in the kitchen, the larder door exploded. Bullets punched splintered holes through it as Scott fired wildly from the inside. Danny instinctively spun away from Red Two and dived behind the kitchen island. Bullets embedding themselves everywhere from the ceiling, to the cupboards to the floor. It was all over in a second. The gun Danny had given Scott clicked empty and silence fell over the kitchen as the dust settled. Danny jumped up to see Red Two still standing in the middle of the kitchen. The SCO19 officer turned slowly, a terrified look on his face as he clutched his throat, blood pumping out between his gloved fingers. With the colour draining from his face, he dropped to his knees, staring at Danny with pleading eyes. Seconds later, his blood pressure bottomed out, his eyes rolled back in his head, and he fell flat on his front in a pool of his own blood.

'You can come out now, Scott,' Danny shouted, moving to the window to check on the imminent arrival of Blue Team.

'Oh my, you killed him,' Scott said, grimacing at the sight of the dead SCO19 officer.

'Don't look at me, Scotty boy, that was all you, mate. You damn near blew my head off.'

'Don't blame me, old man. You're the one who said if anyone other than you comes into the kitchen, start shooting,' Scott replied indignantly. 'I say, Tobias, isn't it?' he continued, turning to look at Tobias at the back of the larder cupboard.

Tobias nodded, his face as white as a sheet, with a look of horror written all over it.

'You might be better off not looking.'

'No, you'd better look. You and your stupid mates caused all this. Did you think about all the people you killed when you blew up the pub in London, or Giles Wright and his family when you had him killed? Well? What about two of my friends you killed just while they were just trying to do their jobs?' Danny snarled, his eyes burning angrily in Tobias's direction.

'That wasn't me. I didn't agree to any of that. I just wanted to disrupt some services and get our message heard. The man we were supposed to meet today, the government man, he arranged the pub bombing and the attack on the NCSC. I just wanted to make the world a better place,' Tobias said, tears streaming from his eyes.

'Yeah, well, how's that working out for you?' Danny snapped back before turning to look out the window.

Danny's eyes went wide and he dropped to the floor, just before the glass imploded under a hail of bullets that tore across the kitchen, obliterating a set of cupboards on the wall opposite.

'Get down! Crawl over here by me, move.'

Danny poked his gun just above the glassless window and

returned fire, slowing the approaching Blue Team as they took cover, buying them some time. Scott grabbed Tobias's arm and dragged him over to the safety of the front wall of the farmhouse.

'Keep close to the wall and go through into the dining room,' Danny yelled, firing out the window again until his gun clicked empty.

Dropping it, Danny turned to follow Scott and Tobias as they shuffled across the dining room on their hands and knees. Something thudded into the kitchen island and rattled to the floor behind him. He looked back to see a stun grenade spinning on the stone floor.

'Shit!' he yelled. He dived and rolled through the doorway into the dining room, kicking the door shut as the stun grenade went off. Even with it shut, the blinding light lit up the dining room from the gaps around the door and the sound wave from the explosion punched through their chests and rattled their brains. Danny fought the effects and shook his head as he stumbled to his feet and made his way to the table, grabbing the Heckler and Koch G36 assault rifle from the Nova South attack.

'Stay behind me,' Danny yelled at the top of his voice, the ringing in his ears from the stun grenade making him temporarily deaf.

He headed into the hall with Scott and Tobias close behind him, pushing the sagging front door forward so it at least blocked the line of sight from outside as it hung at forty-five degrees across the doorway.

'Up, up,' he said quieter than before, the ringing in his ears dying off a little.

As Danny backed up the stairs, shadows danced on the floor from two of Blue Team crossing in front of the dining room window. Danny let off a short burst of fire through the open doorway to keep them back. In the following silence,

Danny heard glass breaking behind the door to the living room as the remaining pair from Blue Team forced their way through the window.

Shit, come on, Simon, now would be a really good time to do something.

CHAPTER 52

'Blue One to Blue Three, we are in position.'

'Blue Three, we are also in position, covering fire on three. One, two, three.'

The second Blue Three poked his rifle and part of his head around the living room door, bullets from Danny's rifle tore razor sharp splinters from the door frame millimetres from his head.

'Fuck, bastard,' Blue Three spun back into the living room, letting his rifle hang on its shoulder strap as he pulled his gloves off and painfully removed several inch-long splinters from his cheek.

'Blue Three, are you alright?' said Blue One, looking at his colleague across the hall from inside the dining room.

Blue Three pulled the last splinter out and put a thumb up to Blue One.

'I'm good. We're going to have to flush this bastard out.'

Upstairs, Danny held his palm up, pushing it forward to tell Scott and Tobias to stay where they were at the rear of the back bedroom. Treading lightly, he left them and made the short distance across the landing to enter the bedroom directly above the dining room. Standing inside, he used the window that lined up with the dining room window below as his point of reference. Moving the rifle in from the window then across the carpet, Danny aimed at the floor, picturing where Blue Team would be standing in the dining room below. With the rifle set to two round bursts, Danny tapped off shots at the floor, working across the room in neat horizontal lines. Bullets ripped down through the carpet and wooden floorboards until an agonising yell came from below.

As soon as Danny heard the cry he ran for the landing. With his partner groaning on the floor, the SCO19 officer still standing opened fire at the ceiling, spraying bullets in every direction until the magazine was empty, hoping that one would kill Danny in the bedroom above. Oblivious to the flying bullets, wood and carpet in the bedroom behind him, Danny's mind was more worried about the incoming fire from the living room. Plaster popped off the landing wall behind his head as he dashed for the back bedroom. He returned fire until his rifle clicked empty, pushing Blue Three back into the living room even though he was moving too fast for an accurate shot. Scott and Tobias looked over as Danny burst into the room and threw the empty rifle on the floor. He looked around for anything he could use to defend them, his eyes settling on the heavy cast iron radiator.

'Scott, give me a hand.'

'Of course,' Scott replied, moving up next to him as he grabbed the radiator, the two of them trying to pull it away from the wall.

When it didn't move, Danny picked the rifle back up and jammed the stock between the radiator and the wall. He placed a foot against the wall as he and Scott tried to lever the radiator off its wall fixing. The brick around the fixings eventually gave way and the radiator lurched forward, stopping at a forty-five degree angle. As it wobbled on the bent heating pipes fixed to each end, Danny kicked and pulled the soft copper pipes until they split and eventually snapped, a gush of dirty black radiator water spraying out of either side until it drained out. With the veins popping on his neck, Danny lifted the heavy cast iron radiator off the ground and staggered towards the landing. As he left the room, three of Blue Team were heading up the stairs. They fired in his direction, the bullets sparking as they ricocheted off the metal radiator. With a roar, Danny hurled it down the stairs at them. It hit a wooden step first, splitting it in half before bouncing and spinning downwards, hitting one of Blue Team in the chest. With the downwards momentum it was like being hit by a truck and knocked him clean off his feet into his two teammates on the way down. Danny didn't wait to see the outcome. Bullets were already ripping lumps out of the bannisters and ceiling above him as he dived back into the bedroom.

'What do we do now?' Scott said, helping his friend up.

'Sorry, Scott, I'm out of ideas,' Danny replied, trying to get his breath back.

At the bottom of the stairs, two of Blue Team picked themselves back up and looked at their colleague lying at the base of the stairs with a broken neck. Determined to get even and kill Danny and the others, they reloaded and started toward the staircase. As Blue One placed a foot onto the first step, the house started shaking and a thunderous whomping sound filled the air. A powerful downdraft blew the front door inward on its broken hinges. Red Four covered his eyes as he lay on the doorstep in pain next to his dead teammate. Leaves and debris flew around and the trees thrashed about on the far side. Ropes dropped into view and members of the 22 SAS rapidly descended from the 658 Squadron support helicopter. A split second later they hit the ground, stepped forward and knelt with rifles up and pointing at members of Red and Blue Teams while more of their unit followed. Within seconds they were all down and the helicopter pulled away.

'Lay your weapons down, now.'

'Get down on the floor, hands behind your heads, do it now,' came the follow-up orders from two advancing soldiers.

'We're SCO19, you have no authority here,' Blue One shouted, trying to take command of the situation.

'I've got authorisation to use deadly force if need be. I advise you not to test me on that. Now lay down your weapon and get on the floor with your hands behind your head,' replied the captain in charge, his men already dragging the members of Red Team from the barn while others entered the farmhouse from all points.

Knowing he was beat, Blue One and his men did as they were ordered while Martin Webster's panicking voice demanded answers over his earpiece.

'Blue Team, what the hell's going on? Come in, Blue Team.'

'Blue One to Command, the game's up,' he said just before the soldiers took the radios from them.

'Clear.'

'Clear.'

'Clear,' came in as the soldiers moved like a well-oiled machine through the downstairs of the farmhouse.

'Mr Pearson, Simon sends his regards. Are you and Mr Miller uninjured?' the captain shouted up the stairs.

Moving slowly into view, Danny looked down at him, covered in oil and black radiator water, his hands up in front of him so he wouldn't be mistaken for a hostile.

'Yeah, we're fine,' Danny said, saluting the captain out of respect.

'Good man. Damn fine job, soldier,' the captain saluted back amongst the destruction of the farmhouse.

'Bloody good timing, chaps,' Scott said, appearing from behind Danny with Tobias not far behind.

CHAPTER 53

In the back of the command vehicle, Martin Webster and the two operators looked at each other while listening to the cacophony of confusing noise from the radios. Webster leaned forward and spoke into the microphone.

'Blue Team, what the hell's going on? Come in, Blue Team,' he demanded.

'Blue One to Command, the game's up,' came back over the top of, 'Get down on the floor, hands behind your heads, do it now,' from the SAS team.

'Er, er, we've got to go. We've got to get out of here, now,' he spluttered, dragging the operator out of his seat and pushing him towards the cab.

Webster got in the passenger seat beside him, doing his seat belt up as the driver spun the wheels to bump and slide the large command vehicle through a three-point turn in the woodland clearing. They sped back along the track, holding onto whatever they could as they hit potholes and humps. The vehicle leaned precariously as the driver turned hard, sliding sideways off the muddy track onto the lane, snaking violently as the tyres flicked off mud before they could get a grip on the tarmac. Webster held onto the armrest with white knuckles, his heart pounding in his chest and mind panicking beyond comprehensible thought, only remembering to breathe when his head started spinning. A mile down the lane, they left the woods and high hedgerows behind, shooting out into the open with only raw ploughed fields on either side. A huge downdraft rocked the van and a cloud of dry dirt whipped up off the fields to pepper the metal bodywork of the command vehicle. The low whomp of rotor blades hit them a second later as a 658 Squadron support helicopter passed over the top of them. It shot forward about half a mile before banking hard to face the approaching command vehicle as it hurtled down the lane. It lowered slowly onto the tarmac in front of them, forcing the driver to bring the command vehicle to a halt.

'Shit, shit, shit,' Webster said, panicking, his finger shaking as he made a call.

'Is it done?' came Birchwood's voice before Webster had a chance to speak.

'No, it's not fucking done. It's very, very fucking far from being done, Alfred,' replied Webster.

'What the hell are you talking about, Martin?'

'We got screwed, there was someone else at the farmhouse, one of Simon's bloody assets. He took out Red Team and half of Blue Team before all hell broke loose. Helicopters, soldiers, it's all gone to shit.'

'Where are you now? Did you get away?'

Webster looked out the windscreen to see Simon step down from the helicopter, immaculately dressed in an expensive suit as always. Three SAS soldiers moved past him, slowly approaching the command vehicle with their rifles pointed at both of them.

'Shit, he's here.'

'Who's there?' Birchwood commanded.

'Simon, he's here. It's all over, Alfred. I'm ruined,' Webster replied, on the brink of tears.

'Listen to me, you little shit. You and your useless team say nothing, you hear me? Nothing. I'll have a team of lawyers with you as soon as I can. We'll say you were acting on an anonymous tip off, ok? They can't prove anything. Just keep that mouth of yours shut and I'll get you out,' Birchwood yelled before hanging up.

Webster took the phone away from his ear, keeping his hands in the air as the soldiers moved to either side of the vehicle, tapping on the glass with the end of their rifles as they ordered them to get out. Webster did as he was told, the soldier pushing him forward in front of the vehicle to face Simon as he approached.

'My, my, Martin, you do seem to be in a dreadful hurry. Why don't you take a little ride with me? I'll have you back in London in no time. There are a quite a few people who'd like a word with you,' Simon said in a loud but jovial voice over the noise of the nearby helicopter. He turned to one side as he gestured towards the helicopter as if inviting Webster for a ride.

The soldier behind Webster nudged him forward. Webster stumbled, then found his feet and walked slowly towards the helicopter, not having the nerve to look Simon in the eye as he passed.

'Would you gentlemen care to take the command vehicle and its crew back to the farmhouse? My agents and the emergency services are on their way to secure the scene and take care of the injured. I would appreciate it if Mr Pearson and Mr Miller were somewhere else by the time they get there,' Simon said to the two remaining SAS soldiers.

'Yes, sir.'

'Thank you,' Simon said, leaving them to head back to the helicopter.

He got in and placed a headset on as he sat next to a sorry-looking Webster. 'London heliport please,' he said into the microphone.

'Yes sir,' came an immediate response from the pilot, the helicopter lifting off the road seconds later.

It gained height fast, circling to fly back over the woods and the farmhouse. The other 658 Squadron support helicopter sitting in the meadow to one side of the farmhouse with its rotor blades still spinning, while the SAS soldiers had everyone either detained or receiving medical attention in the courtyard. They were to keep the area contained until Simon's men arrived, then make a rapid exit via helicopter before the media got wind of anything. Simon smiled to himself at the sight of Danny and Scott standing next to the captain, looking up as he flew over.

'ETA please,' Simon said, taking his phone out.

'Approximately thirty minutes, sir,' came the pilot's voice over the headphones.

'Thank you,' Simon replied politely, sending a message to make sure they were met on arrival.

Taking another headset off a hook behind the seat, Simon handed it to Webster, who reluctantly took it and put it on.

'Martin, how about we have a little chat about Alfred Birchwood?'

'No, no, I'm saying nothing without a lawyer. I've done nothing wrong,' Webster blurted out, his eyes darting around the helicopter, looking anywhere other than meeting Simon's unwavering stare.

'Now, I think we both know that's not true, don't we, Martin?' Simon said calmly.

'I refuse to say a word until I have my lawyer present,' Webster said with more confidence as he convinced himself that Birchwood would take care of things and protect him.

Simon remained relaxed, giving Webster a smile before answering. 'That's not the way this works Martin,' he said, turning to the soldier sitting opposite them. 'Sergeant, would you mind showing our guest out?'

'Yes sir.'

The sergeant slid the door of the helicopter back and grabbed Webster, pulling him out of his seat so fast the headset fell off his head. He shoved Webster to the floor on his front and gripped the back of his suit jacked tightly in his hands, shoving Webster forward so that his top half was out the helicopter door. He screamed as the trees whizzed by below him before begging.

'Stop, please, stop. I'll tell you everything. Please stop,' he yelled through the sobs.

The sergeant held Webster in place, making him suffer until Simon gave him the nod, and he yanked him back inside, dumping him back in the seat before sliding the helicopter door shut. Webster flinched through the tears as Simon leaned towards him. When he got close, he reached down and picked up the headset and handed it to him. Reluctantly, Webster took the headset and put it on, his hands shaking violently as he placed it over his ears.

'Now that you have had some fresh air and a chance to think, shall we start again? Tell me everything you know about Alfred Birchwood,' Simon continued, the charismatic smile never leaving his face.

CHAPTER 54

irchwood slammed his phone down on the desk next to his keyboard. He leapt up out of his office chair and paced around the room. Returning to his desk, Birchwood picked up the phone and called Temple. It rang several times before clicking to voicemail. He was about to leave a message, but stopped and hung up instead.

What if Temple's phone was already in the hands of the authorities?

Paranoia and fear crept into his thoughts. He got up and moved over to the window, tilting the wooden slats to look through the blinds at his drive and the road beyond. There were no police cars, no men in dark suits. He breathed a sigh of relief and dialled the number for Birchwood McMillan Security.

'Er, Birchwood McMillan Security,' came the receptionist's unusually strained reply.

'It's Alfred Birchwood. I need to speak to Mr Temple,' he ordered abruptly.

'Oh, Mr Birchwood, I'm afraid you can't. The police and lots of men in suits are here. They took Nick, Matt and Darren away and we've been ordered to stop what we're doing.

They're taking all the files and computers away. I don't know what to—'

Birchwood hung up without letting her finish, his mind racing as he tried to get a grip on the situation.

I've got to get away, I've got money, I can get a new identity, start a new life.

Jolted into action, Birchwood turned on his computer screens and logged into his legitimate bank accounts. Starting with the seventy-five million sitting in the Birchwood Technologies business account, he transferred every penny he had into a selection of offshore accounts. Taking his eye off the screens, Birchwood glanced out the window, relieved to see that there were no police cars screaming up the drive. Focusing back on the computer, Birchwood's fingers moved like lightning over the keys as he transferred large lumps of money from the offshore accounts into various shell company accounts around the world, making the money trail impossible to follow. When he'd finished he went into a special program he'd written himself and hit the destroy all button. A bar appeared and moved across the screen, counting steadily up to one hundred. On the final count, his computer died and the screens went black. The fans and lights in the six-foot-high cabinet housing his computer system faded and spun to a halt. Birchwood fetched his passport and a few documents from the drawer in his desk and ran upstairs with the phone to his ear.

'London City Airport private jet centre.'

'Good afternoon, this is Alfred Birchwood. I have an account with you and require a jet today, as soon as possible.'

'Certainly, Mr Birchwood, where would you like to go?'

'To Geneva International Airport,' Birchwood said, putting the phone on speaker as he threw it on the bed and headed for the wardrobe. He grabbed a small suitcase from inside and frantically started packing it with clothes.

'Of course, Mr Birchwood, we have a Gulfstream available. Would you like me to price that up for you?'

'No, no need, just charge my account, whatever it costs. I'll be with you in about an hour.'

'Certainly, sir, we'll have the plane prepped and ready for your arrival.'

Birchwood wasn't listening. He grabbed his bag and phone and ran down the stairs to the front door. He froze with his hand on the latch, panic gripping him. Moving to the side, Birchwood looked out across the drive and road for a third time. With the sound of his own heart thumping in his ears, he stood rooted to the spot, expecting a stream of police cars to swerve through the gates and up to the house at any moment. His head spun and his lungs burned, the extreme stress making him forget to breathe. Forcing himself to move, he sucked in great gulps of air and yanked the front door open before running to his car. He threw the suitcase on the passenger seat, started the engine before speeding out of the drive. With his foot down on the accelerator, Birchwood flew along the road at over twice its thirty miles an hour speed limit, setting off a speed camera as he tried to put as much distance away from his house as possible. By the time he turned down the slip road onto the M11, Birchwood's breathing returned to normal and his thoughts focused on self preservation.

I have money, lots of money. When I get to Geneva, I'll get some plastic surgery done, buy a new face and a new identity. I can start again somewhere new, South Africa perhaps. You can't keep me down, I can do anything I want.

CHAPTER 55

'**M**r Pearson. Orders from Simon, you and Mr Miller are to make yourselves scarce and look lively about it. We've got inbound. Ten minutes from now this place is going to be crawling with agents and police,' the SAS captain said, getting everything ready to hand the crime scene over and evacuate by helicopter the second Simon's men arrived.

'Thank you, Captain, I'm glad you arrived when you did. I owe you one,' Danny replied, shaking the captain's hand.

'It was our pleasure. You're somewhat of a legend in The Regiment. I'm glad to see you're still living up to your reputation,' the captain said, giving a nod to Danny before heading back to the troops.

'Time to go, Scotty boy.'

'What? Oh right, yes. Lead the way, old man.'

Danny jogged across the courtyard and pushed through the tree line into the woods. He headed in a straight line towards the country lane, smiling to himself as Scott grumbled at the twigs and low-hanging branches that sprang back to hit him in the face and body.

'Ouch, bloody hell, you did that on purpose.'

'Sorry, Scott, did you say something?'

'Yes, ok, very funny.'

'Down,' Danny said, suddenly serious as he dropped into a crouch behind the trunk of a tree.

Scott tucked in behind him, both of them looking out at the lane from under cover while the sound of sirens grew ever louder. There was a rush of wind and the noise peaked as Simon's men and police cars and ambulances, and even a fire engine hurtled past. Danny and Scott stayed out of sight until the last stragglers had sped past, then emerged from the tree line and ran the short distance to the field where Danny had parked the car. He opened the boot, grateful that his gym bag was still inside. Stripping out of his oil and dirt covered clothes, Danny used a towel from the gym bag to scrub as much grime off his face and hands as he could, before pulling a pair of shorts and a T-shirt on. He chucked the dirty clothes and his gun in the boot and slammed it shut before getting in.

'Ready to go home, Scotty?'

'Absolutely. You'd better give Nikki a call and let her know we're ok.'

'I will, let's just get away from here first,' Danny said, reversing the car out through the gap in the hedge, bumping it down onto the tarmac before driving off. He kept under the speed limit and worked his way through the country lanes until he hit the main road, calling Nikki as they joined the M11 and headed towards London.

'Danny, are you alright?' came Nikki's worried voice over the car's speakers.

'Yes, love, I'm fine, not a scratch. I've got somebody here who wants to say hello.'

'Hello, sis, I'm fine as well,' said Scott from the passenger seat.

'Oh god, I'm so relieved,' Nikki blurted out before bursting into tears of relief.

'Hey, hey, there's no need for that. I said we're ok. Genesis

UK turned out to be a bunch of misguided kids. I found their location and got Simon to get his guys in. We're on our way home now,' Danny said, underplaying all the details to reassure Nikki, while Scott shook his head at him for lying.

'Ok, I'll see you soon, love you,' Nikki said, pulling herself together.

'What's that look for?' Danny said to Scott once Nikki was off the phone.

'You shouldn't lie to her.'

'Yeah, I know, but you heard her. She was really upset. We're safe and sound. What good would it do telling her all the gory details? She's been really emotional lately.'

'Ok, my lips are sealed, but I'm just saying these things have a habit of coming out.'

'Right, well, next time I won't bother saving your sorry arse,' Danny said grumpily.

'Are we sulking now, really? Oh, and thank you for saving my sorry arse by the way. It was much appreciated,' Scott said sarcastically, which made Danny chuckle and lifted the mood in the car.

'Come back to ours. Nikki will want to see you. You can have a shower and something to eat with a few beers. I'll take you home in the morning.'

'I've got nothing to wear but this ruined suit,' Scott protested, looking down in disgust at his crumpled Armani suit.

'You can borrow some of my clothes.'

'Your clothes? Oh god, hand me back to the kidnappers,' Scott said with a big grin on his face.

'Shut up, you tart,' Danny laughed before adding, 'But seriously, don't start telling your sister all the gory details from the farmhouse, ok?'

'Ok, ok, mum's the word.'

Traffic was light on the journey home and in less than an hour they pulled up outside Danny's house. When he opened the front door Nikki ran through from the kitchen, jumping up to hug him tightly around his neck before kissing him passionately.

'Whoa, easy, love, if I thought I was going to get this reception I'd stay out all night more often,' Danny said as she released him and went to hug her brother.

'Alright, sis, don't fuss, I'm fine.'

'Sorry, I just had this horrible feeling something bad had happened to both of you,' Nikki said, the tears welling up in her eyes again.

'Well, we're home now, safe and sound, so you can relax. All I need is a hot shower, clean clothes and a beer and everything will be right with the world,' Danny said, giving Nikki another kiss before heading upstairs. 'I'll get you a towel and some clothes, mate, you can use the main bathroom, I'll take a shower in the en-suite.'

'Thank you, I'll be right up,' Scott said, hanging back to talk to Nikki. 'Are you ok, sis? You're not usually this, er, emotional when the caveman comes back from one of his little trips.'

'I know, I'm sorry. My head's been all over the place lately. My emotions are up and down like a yo-yo. Look, I'm fine. I'm just glad to have you both back. Go on, go and get a shower.'

Scott smiled at Nikki, gave her another hug and went upstairs to get cleaned up.

CHAPTER 56

A week passed and normality returned to people's lives. The media, as media does, moved on from the excitement of Genesis UK's assault on the establishment, focusing on flooding in one country and a drought in another, as well as the latest nation to declare war on its neighbour. Thankfully for Danny, Simon and the government's press office had suppressed most of the details regarding the downfall of Genesis UK, so he hadn't had to explain what really happened at the farmhouse to Nikki.

The front doorbell rang while he was in the kitchen. He smiled to himself when he heard Nikki greeting his sister-in-law Tina, followed by the tiny footsteps and excited giggles of his niece Sophie running down the hall to find him.

'Uncle Danny,' she shrieked, throwing her arms wide as she jumped up at him.

'Hello kiddo,' Danny grinned, picking her up and spinning her around.

He carried her, still giggling, through to the hall to say hello to Tina.

'Alright Tina, how's the baby?' Danny said, looking in at his sleeping nephew in the pram.

'He's hard work, but at least he's sleeping through the night now.'

'That's good. Where are you two off to today?'

'We're off to Stratford. Nikki's going to spend all your money at Westfield shopping centre.'

'All my money? Well, that'll take you about ten minutes.'

'You see, Tina, I told you I had lousy taste in men,' Nikki laughed, her face dropping as she rubbed her belly.

'She's right, I wouldn't marry me either,' Danny replied, his face turning serious. 'Are you still feeling off?'

'Yeah, a bit. It's just a bug. It'll pass in a minute.'

'Ok, well just take it easy,' Danny said before turning his attention back to Sophie. 'What about you, madam, you want to go shopping with mummy and auntie Nikki, or do you want to come to the sweaty gym and work out with Uncle Danny?'

Sophie screwed her face up and giggled. 'Yuk, go shopping with mummy.'

'Well, you have a good time. I'll see you later,' Danny said, putting Sophie down to give Nikki a kiss goodbye.

They headed out the door and Danny turned to fetch his cup of tea from the kitchen. A knock at the door stopped him just before he picked it up.

'Don't tell me you've forgotten your keys again,' he muttered, spinning on his heels to head back to the door. He pulled it open expecting to see Nikki on the other side instead of Simon standing on his doorstep.

'Good morning, Daniel, I thought I'd try the door this time. I seem to remember you threatened to shoot me the last time I let myself in,' Simon said, his voice smooth as always.

Danny's dislike of Simon had diminished somewhat after his help with getting Scott back, so to Simon's surprise, he just turned his back on him and headed for the kitchen.

'Come in. Tea, coffee?' he said over his shoulder.

'Tea, one sugar,' Simon answered, turning to give a nod to his driver before entering and closing the door behind him.

'I see Martin Webster got off with a resignation,' Danny said, pointing to the news on the TV in the lounge as he passed.

'That was not my doing. The PM's spin doctors deemed it too damaging to the government and the country for the Minister for Security to be put on trial for fraud, corruption, and murder. So they offered him a way out.'

'That's more than the slimy shit deserves,' Danny said, clicking the kettle on.

'He didn't get away totally scot-free. He's been sacked as Minister for Security and removed from the party. His wife has left him and with no one to bolster up his failing business ventures, Mr Webster has been forced into bankruptcy. His assets have been seized and houses taken away. He'll likely be living in a council flat in Peckham by the end of the week,' Simon replied, taking a seat at Danny's kitchen table.

'That's still too good for him.'

'I agree, but His Majesty's government pays my wages, so whatever they say goes.'

'What about Alfred Birchwood?' Danny said, changing the subject.

'Ah, Mr Birchwood and the seventy-five million pounds of taxpayers' money. I have a very special team tracking down Mr Birchwood. That investigation should be coming to a conclusion in the not too distant future,' Simon replied with a slight smile as he took a sip of tea.

'Mmm, well, as pleasant as this is, I'm sure you didn't just pop in for a friendly chat. What do you want, Simon?' Danny said, his facial expression turning serious.

'No, I didn't. We have found our American friend.'

'Where?' Danny said, cutting in.

'A little town near Venice, Italy.'

'Has he been arrested?'

'No, and nor will he be. Our American, real name Oliver Johnson, was a high level asset for the CIA and has operational knowledge that neither side would wish to become public. It's been decided that it is in the best interest of the United States and Great Britain if Mr Johnson was taken care of, discreetly. A collaborative venture with a small two man team. The American representative is already here in London and as promised, I'm offering you the position of second man, for Thomas Trent and John Ball.'

The muscles in Danny's jaw set like stone and a darkness edged into his stare.

'When?'

'There's no time like the present. I have a car waiting and our friends from the US Air Force have laid on a transport plane.'

Danny didn't say anything for a while. Thoughts of the two friends he'd lost at the hands of the American spun around in his head. He knew Nikki wouldn't be happy with him going, but with the death of his friends and the image of Johnson stuck in his head, Danny just couldn't walk away from it. He drained the last of his tea from his mug.

'Let's go,' he finally said, thumping the empty mug down on the table.

Several miles away in Stratford's Westfield shopping centre, Nikki held Sophie's tiny little hand in hers while Tina manoeuvred the pram around the rails of hanging baby clothes.

'Ah, that's so cute, what do you think, Georgie?' Nikki said, holding the outfit up against the gurgling baby.

'I think he likes it, Nikki, give it here, I'll get it for him.'

A wave of emotion hit Nikki as she looked at George and her little niece, Sophie. Her eyes filled with tears and she had to fight to stop sobbing in the middle of the shop.

'Hey, what's wrong? Is everything alright with you and Danny?'

'Sorry, yes, everything's fine. I don't know what's wrong with me. I'm all over the place lately,' Nikki said, drying her eyes and shaking the emotion away.

'I don't know, emotions all over the place, feeling sick for no reason. You're not pregnant, are you?'

'No, don't be silly,' Nikki replied, the confidence in her answer fading as she said it out loud.

'Are you sure?'

'What's the date today?'

'It's the twelfth today,' Tina said, watching Nikki's face drop.

'Oh god, I'm late on.'

There was a pause while Tina tried to gauge whether Nikki being pregnant was something she'd be happy or sad about. The excited grin spreading across Nikki's face told her everything she needed to know.

'Quick, let's go to the chemist and find out.'

With the shopping trip cut short, Tina dropped Nikki home.

'Do you want me to come in?' Tina said.

'No, I'll call you later,' Nikki called back from the front door.

'Ok, good luck.'

'Danny, Danny, where are you? I've got something to tell you,' she shouted as she entered the house, moving through the rooms when he didn't answer.

When he wasn't in the bedroom, Nikki took out her phone and called his number, a frown crossing her face when she heard it ring somewhere downstairs. She followed the sound and found Danny's mobile sitting on top of a note on the kitchen table.

Sorry, love, there's something I have to do for Tom and John. I'll be home as soon as I can. I love you.

Nikki read the note and found herself welling up again.

'Bloody hell, Danny, where are you?' she cried, screwing up the note and throwing it in the bin.

CHAPTER 57

The guards were expecting Simon's car when it arrived at the security gates. A military police jeep escorted them to a nearby building where two MPs escorted them into a room where two people sat waiting.

'Daniel, this is Navy Seal Chief Petty Officer Lucus Delaware and Senior CIA Representative for the UK Hank Samson,' Simon said, as the group took a seat in the small briefing room on the United States Air Force base at Mildenhall in Suffolk.

Danny nodded to Hank and shook Lucus's hand. The way the confident younger man shook then turned away dismissively did not go unnoticed. The attention in the room focused on Hank as he stood up and passed a file to each of them.

'Gentlemen, apologies for the short notice given to prepare you for this operation, but our target is one slippery son of a bitch, and there's no telling how long he will be at his current location.'

'Which is?' said Danny.

'Somewhere near the town of Punta Sabbioni, Venice.'

Hank pulled out a series of blown-up photographs of Oliver Johnson looking relaxed in a T-shirt, shorts and dark glasses as he entered a small supermarket. There were more photos of him wearing similar clothes while drinking coffee in a local cafe and picking fruit from a market stall. 'One of our contacts took these photographs over the course of last week. Johnson travels into town every couple of days, which would suggest he is staying close by. We want you to go to Punta Sabbioni, liaise with our contact and find out where Johnson is staying. When you do, we want you to neutralise him. No messing about. Get in, get it done and get back to Aviano US Air Base where a transport plane will be waiting to bring you home. Is that clear?'

'No problem,' Lucus said confidently while staring at Danny, trying to intimidate him.

Danny was on the verge of declining the job and going home, but Tom and John had both saved his life, Tom several times. He couldn't shake the image in his head of them dying at the hands of Johnson. Justice had to be done so he gave a short, 'Ok.'

'Good, the contact's name is Nico Bernardi. His details are in the file. He will meet you at the Hotel La Rondine in Punta Sabbioni. Let him know what equipment you need and he'll source it for you. Any questions?'

When no one answered, Hank gathered up the photographs and put them in his folder.

'I have an unregistered phone for each of you. The number for each other and an emergency number where you can contact myself or Simon are stored in the contacts. Your flight to Aviano US Air Base leaves in twenty minutes, gentlemen, and if there are no more questions I wish you good luck. Don't underestimate Oliver Johnson. He's a very resourceful and extremely dangerous man.'

With that, Hank opened the briefing room door and called the MPs waiting patiently in the corridor to escort Danny and

Lucus to their waiting transport plane. Minutes later they jumped down from the jeep and entered the cavernous cargo plane, taking a seat along one side. Apart from piles of supplies strapped down along the centre of the cargo hold, Danny and Lucus were the only passengers. As the large cargo door shut and the engines got louder, Lucus turned to Danny.

'Look, we do this my way. Ok? I don't need some retired old soldier getting in the way and screwing this up. When we find Johnson, you're strictly backup. I'll take care of him.'

Danny resisted the urge to punch Lucus's lights out and said nothing. As the engine noise increased, he put his head back against the side of the plane and shut his eyes, trying to sleep the flight away. They landed three hours later without further conversation, the large cargo door opening to let in a blast of late afternoon heat. As they walked down the ramp, a Humvee pulled up and a soldier got out, quickly snapping to attention, and saluting them.

'No need to salute me, mate. I'm a civilian,' Danny said, walking over to him.

'Sorry, sir, I have your vehicle ready and security passes to get you on and off the base.'

'Thanks. Is there anywhere I can get a coffee around here?' Danny added before Lucus barged past him.

'No time. We've got to get going. Can you show us to the vehicle?'

'Yes sir, right this way.'

They got into the Humvee and the driver took them across the base to the motor pool. They pulled up alongside a row of Humvees, trucks and other military vehicles with a grey Nissan Qashqai parked like the odd one out in the middle.

'That's yours. It's fuelled up and ready to go,' the officer said, handing the keys towards Danny, only to have Lucus snatch them from him.

'Let's go,' Lucus said abruptly, not waiting for a response before opening the door and getting out of the Humvee.

'Thank you, er…?'

'Brooks, sir, Lieutenant Kyle Brooks.'

'Well thank you, Lieutenant Brooks,' Danny said with a smile before getting out and heading over to Lucus who was already in the car.

As soon as Danny got in Lucus drove across the base to the main gate, leaving at speed after showing their passes and turning onto the Italian road, following the sat nav for the hour and a half journey to Punta Sabbioni.

They arrived at the hotel around seven. Danny grabbed his rucksack and got out of the car, walking away from Lucus towards the hotel entrance without waiting for him.

'Hey, where are you going?' Lucus shouted after him.

'I've been listening to your shit all day. I'm going to get a beer and something to eat. You can either join me or throw yourself under a bus. Quite frankly I couldn't give a shit which.'

'Pearson, come back here, I'm ordering you,' Lucus bellowed.

'I'm a civilian, dickhead. You can't order me to do jack shit,' Danny replied, throwing his arm up to give Lucus the middle finger before disappearing inside the hotel.

Completely thrown by the answer, Lucus stood by the car not knowing what to do. After a minute he gave in, grabbed his bag and followed Danny inside. When he got to the bar, Danny turned and smiled at him before sliding one of the two beers he'd ordered towards him.

'Right, how about we start again?' he said.

Lucus took a minute then his face finally relaxed. He picked up the beer and took a big gulp.

'Thanks.'

'You're welcome. Now, let's order some food and eat, then we can give this Nico a call.'

'No need, my friends, I'm sitting right next to you,' came a voice from the end of the bar.

They both turned to see a small wiry Italian smiling back at them.

'You eaten, Nico?' Danny said with a smile.

CHAPTER 58

Danny woke up the next morning, scratched his head, and wiped the slightly hungover sleep out of his eyes. He checked the time on his trusty G-Shock watch and forced himself out of bed and into the shower. By the time he got down to the dining room, Nico and Lucus already had a table and were tucking into croissants, pastries and thick strong cappuccinos. Seeing that there was no English breakfast on the menu, Danny joined them with the croissants and pastries, swilling them down with strong coffee.

'Damn, that clears the head,' Danny said, looking into the empty coffee cup.

'Ah, to me that is mild. You English drink coffee that tastes like dishwater,' Nico piped up with a smile.

'You might be right, Nico, my old mate, but I probably won't sleep for a week after this stuff,' Danny said, tipping the empty cappuccino cup in Nico's direction.

'Hey, can we get down to business?' Lucus interrupted impatiently.

Danny and Nico looked across the table at Lucus but refrained from making any comment.

'Ok, Nico. You have the items we asked for last night?'

'Yes, for the rifles I got Beretta AR70/90s and for the hand-guns I have two Beretta 92FS semi-automatic pistols. They are in the boot of my car,' Nico said quietly while looking around the dining room.

'Good, and you'll show us the locations in the photos, where you've seen Johnson?' Lucus added.

'Yes, I will show you, then the rest is up to you.'

'That's fine, thank you, Nico,' Danny said, the three of them getting up to leave the dining hall.

In a corner of the car park, Danny and Lucus moved the firearms from Nico's car into their Nissan Qashqai. They put the rifles in the boot while tucking the Beretta 92FS pistols into the back of their jeans, hiding them from view under their light jackets. They followed Nico into the town centre, parking up near the cafe where Nico had seen Johnson on two separate occasions.

'That is the cafe. If you walk straight down there for about half a kilometre you will come across the small supermarket with the market stalls running down the road to the left. That's me done. Good luck, gentlemen.'

'Thank you, Nico,' Danny said while Lucus nodded and waved him off.

'So how do you want to play this?' Danny said, letting Lucus take the lead.

'It could be days until he shows again and we can't afford to miss him at one place if we're both sitting at the other. I say we split and watch the cafe and the market. If one of us sees Johnson, we call the other.'

'I agree. You stay here. I'll take a walk down the road and check out the market,' Danny said, much to Lucus's surprise. He stepped out of the car, leaning back in before he headed off. 'I'm not trying to teach you to suck eggs, but if you see Johnson, keep well back, the slightest whiff that he's being followed and he'll be gone.'

'I hear you, I'll be careful,' Lucus said, giving Danny a nod as he shut the door and headed off towards the market.

Danny looked around Punta Sabbioni as he walked. It was warm and friendly, with neat white-washed buildings with red clay roof tiles. It wouldn't be a bad place to live. He reached the small supermarket and went in, looking around at the products on sale - fresh produce, meats, cheeses, and items you would take home to cook for your evening meal. Not the sort of shop a man on the run would grab something quick from. He bought an apple and left the shop, turning to walk through the market while he took bites out of it. Stopping at one of the little stalls, Danny bought a classic Italian hat made from light straw to look more in keeping with the locals, and to keep the hot sun off his head. He added a pair of sunglasses from another stall before walking back out of the market to survey the road.

There was another cafe around twenty metres away on the opposite side of the road. Danny crossed over and made his way to it. He sat down and ordered a coffee, picking up an Italian newspaper left on the table by a previous customer. Holding it up, he tilted his head slightly forward. From a distance it looked like he was reading, while he looked over the top of it at the little supermarket and the entrance to the market.

The morning dragged its way into the afternoon. He called Lucus around 2pm and they swapped places. Danny sat in the hot sweaty car and watched the cafe until the sun went down. By nine o'clock they called it a day and returned to the hotel. They ordered some food and had a couple of drinks, chatting about various adventures in each other's lives before turning in for the night, ready to do it all again the next day.

CHAPTER 59

59

Like a scene in the film Groundhog Day, Danny and Lucus took up the same positions as the day before. Danny sat in the same chair, in the same cafe, drinking a cup of extremely strong coffee while pretending to read the Italian newspaper he'd kept with him from yesterday. The waitress found it strange, but didn't care enough to worry about a customer who couldn't speak Italian sitting for hours sipping coffee with a paper he couldn't read.

Parked down the road, Lucus sat in the car. The temperature was already rising, causing beads of sweat to trickle down his face as he watched the cafe opposite. His legs cramped, so he got out and walked up and down the pavement beside the car to stretch them out. When he looked up, a silver Mercedes had pulled up on the opposite side of the road next to the cafe. Oliver Johnson got out. He moved forward towards the cafe, his head turning casually in Lucus's direction. Trying to look like a local, Lucus turned away and held his phone like he was reading a message. When he looked back at the cafe, Johnson was staring straight at him like an apex predator eyeing his meal. The moment only lasted a second, but it was obvious he'd made Lucus. Johnson spun on his heels and got back in the Mercedes. Lucus pulled the door open and jumped into the Qashqai, both cars starting their engines at the same time. Lucus hit the call button on his phone, leaving it on speaker as he slammed the car into gear and screamed off after Johnson.

'Yep,' Danny said, leaning to one side to look around a delivery van blocking his view of the market as it dropped bread off at the cafe.

'Johnson's here. He's made me. I'm giving chase,' came Lucus's raised voice over the sound of him pushing the Qashqai to the max.

'Where are you?' Danny said, his question answered as the Mercedes, followed by Lucus, flew past the front of the cafe. 'Don't you lose him. I'm on my way.'

Jumping out of his seat, Danny threw the hat off his head and ran to the driver's side of the delivery van. As he hoped, the keys were still in it. He jumped in and started it, tearing off as the driver ran out of the cafe yelling and shaking his fists, a trail of loaves and baguettes tumbling across the road from the open back doors.

'He's just turned right by a pizza restaurant,' Lucas yelled over the sound of screeching tyres.

'I see it, keep on him, Lucus,' Danny shouted to his phone on the passenger seat.

The van was old, heavy, and sluggish. It cornered badly, snaking as Danny struggled to straighten up, the back doors banging from shut to fully open as they swung around with the movement of the van.

'He's turned by Boschetto camping village. I think he's heading towards the beach,' came through Danny's phone, the sound of the rattling diesel engine making it hard to hear.

'Keep with him,' Danny shouted, not sure how far behind he was.

'Shit, I've lost him. No wait, I see his car. It's parked by a large villa near the beach. I'm going in,' said Lucus, his voice clear now that the car was stationary, blocking the long drive to the villa.

'No, Lucus, do not go in there. Wait for me. Lucus!' Danny shouted, thumping the steering wheel in frustration.

'I've left the rifle and gun in the boot. Follow me in when you get here.'

'Lucus, Lucus. Wait for me, I'll be two minutes, Lucus. Fuck,' Danny shouted as Lucus hung up.

Danny spotted the camping village up ahead and hit the brakes to make the turn, both rear doors banging shut as the van slowed and leaned precariously as it turned. A minute later he pulled up behind the Qashqai, blocking Johnson from leaving. Danny got out and opened the car boot, he grabbed the Beretta AR70/90 assault rifle and headed up the drive, moving from the cover of one tree to another as he approached the villa.

Why has he come here? Why didn't he just shake Lucas and keep running? It doesn't make sense.

CHAPTER 60

Lucus entered the villa around the back by the swimming pool. The large patio doors were already open, allowing him to enter the kitchen silently, his eyes looking along the rifle sights as he moved towards an arch leading into the dining room. He felt the trip wire across his ankle as he stepped through it. Looking down, Lucus saw a metal pin tied to the end of the wire ping loose from a stun grenade taped to one side of the arch. His brain didn't have time to process it before the stun grenade exploded in a blinding white light and a deafening bang. With his eyesight starred out like he'd looked at the sun and a whistling deafness in his ears, Lucus spun in panic, firing his rifle in all directions for fear that Johnson would attack him while defenceless. His fears were confirmed when the rifle clicked empty. Johnson burst through a door on the far side of the kitchen, firing at Lucus as he stumbled blindly backwards, tripping and falling over a small table in the lounge. A shot meant for Lucus's forehead missed its target as he fell, tearing a hole through his ear, while the shot meant for his heart ripped into his shoulder.

Lucus landed flat on his back away from the arch, disappearing from Johnson's sight behind the dining room wall. As Johnson crossed the kitchen to finish Lucus off, shadows and disrupted sunlight from outside made him turn to see Danny's silhouette spinning in from the side of the villa, his rifle pointing in Johnson's direction. With lightning reactions, Johnson changed direction, bullets drawing in a line in the wall behind his head as he bolted out of the kitchen. Keeping the door where Johnson exited covered, Danny stepped sideways across the kitchen before stepping back through the arch. He knelt down next to Lucus, checking there was no sign of Johnson before laying his rifle down and ripping Lucus's shirt open to check his shoulder wound. It was bleeding but not at a flow that would suggest an arterial bleed.

'Is it bad?' Lucus grunted in pain as Danny rolled him to the side to check the exit wound.

'Nah, it's just a scratch, mate. Just hang on there a minute,' Danny said, laying him back down gently.

He ducked back into the kitchen and riffled through the drawers until he found some cleaning cloths and a roll of cling film. Taking them back to Lucus, he helped him up into a sitting position against the arch. Danny applied pressure to the wound with the cloths before winding the cling film under his arm and over the shoulder, then around his chest to keep the pressure on the wound and the cloths in place.

'You'll be ok. Here, take this. Can you see alright?' Danny said, putting his rifle in Lucus's good hand.

'Yeah just, it's coming back,' Lucus said loudly over the whistling in his ears.

'Good, I'm going after him. If he doubles back this way, you take the bastard out, ok?'

Lucus nodded, his body shaking as it went into shock from being shot.

Danny drew the Beretta 92F pistol from the back of his trousers and headed through the open door after Johnson.

The passageway led out into a courtyard with a covered walkway around the outside, big stone pillars lined the square supporting the first floor of the villa above it. Danny moved in close behind a pillar, breathing steadily to lower his heart rate and take the time to read his surroundings. Taking a quick peep out from either side of his pillar, Danny moved around it and headed forward on his toes to tuck in behind the next one. He stopped and listened again. The wait was excruciating. A minute felt like an hour, but eventually there it was, the slight scrape of a shoe on the rough tiled floor. Hard to tell exactly how close, but it was close.

Danny darted a look around the pillar, then repeated the action on the other side, catching the briefest glimpse of brown hair as Johnson tucked in behind the next pillar in front of him. Moving fast, Danny whipped his head and gun around the other side of the pillar, taking a shot and blowing a lump of masonry out just above Johnson's head as he pulled back under cover. Spinning out the other side, Danny charged forward, Johnson mirroring his movements to do the same, as if they were in a choreographed dance. Both men grabbed the other's wrist with their left hand and pushed the other's gun up away from their head.

Johnson twisted in, lifting his leg to drive a knee into Danny's side, repeating the move again in quick succession. Winded but suddenly consumed by so much rage he didn't feel the pain, Danny threw his head forward and headbutted Johnson on the bridge of his nose. Using Johnson's temporary disorientation, Danny smacked his hand against the pillar until he released the gun, letting it fly into the plant beds in the middle of the courtyard. With blood running down from his nose and across his gritted teeth, Johnson bent his knees and let go of Danny's wrist to grip him behind his back. He lifted Danny clean off his feet, roaring as he charged forward and slammed Danny into the stone pillar behind.

Pain shot down Danny's spine, the air left his lungs and

the gun flew from his hand. Johnson stepped back and started powering blows into Danny's body. Danny crumpled and his head started swimming as his legs gave way, dropping him to his knees while still trying to fend off the blows. Seeing victory within his grasp, Johnson swung his bent leg in to power a rock-hard knee into Danny's face. Dodging to one side, Danny grabbed Johnson's leg and launched himself up, lifting him off his feet before smacking Johnson down onto the stone floor.

The fighting didn't let up for a second. Johnson blocked and punched as Danny knelt over him doing the same. Drawing his foot back, Johnson kicked Danny off him, immediately lunging forward to wrap his arm around Danny's neck, grabbing his own wrist with his other hand to pull the arm tighter in a chokehold. Danny fought hard, digging his elbow into Johnson's ribs as he tried to twist out of the hold. But try as he might, he couldn't breathe and couldn't break free.

With his head spinning, Danny caught sight of his Beretta pistol lying on the stone floor. Stretching his arm out, his fingers scratched across the stone floor as he tried to get a grip on the butt of the gun. His vision blurred and darkness started to creep in. He felt a finger touch the butt of the gun. With his last ounce of strength, he stretched across the extra inch and got a grip on it. Pulling it in, Danny swung it across his chest and aimed it around his side at Johnson, pulling the trigger.

In his semi-conscious state, Danny heard a groan and the pressure on his neck disappeared. He rolled on his front, sucking in great gulps of air. When his vision cleared, he saw Johnson limping back into the villa while holding his side, blood oozing between his fingers and staining his white T-shirt. Danny forced himself to his feet and staggered after him.

CHAPTER 61

Following Johnson, Danny found himself in the hall. He moved towards the front door, expecting Johnson to have made his escape that way. Danny stopped when the droplets of blood on the floor headed off in a different direction. He turned to see a bloody handprint on the wall by the base of the stairs. A painful groan and shuffling movement from somewhere on the first floor confirming Johnson's whereabouts.

Why didn't he make a run for it?

With his breathing returned to normal, Danny moved up the stairs, his arm locked out in front of him. He moved with the gun up in front of him, the drops of blood stopping outside an open bedroom door in front of him. Tucking in beside the door, Danny darted his head across to see into the bedroom. Johnson was rifling through a set of drawers, holding a folded up towel on the bullet wound to his side as he threw clothes out of the way. Seeing the butt of a gun appearing from one of the drawers, Danny charged inside and punched Johnson on top of the bullet wound. Gripped with pain, Johnson dropped the gun and crumpled to the floor in agony. Danny stepped forward, locking his gun onto the centre of Johnson's forehead as he prepared to fire. A young boy with black curly hair and dark brown eyes ran out from the en-suite bathroom screaming, 'Papa,' before throwing his arms around Johnson. The boy's mother followed the boy out from the en-suite bathroom, tears streaming from her eyes as she called the boy back.

'Maria, take the boy,' Johnson said, trying to push him away without taking his eyes off Danny.

Danny watched her drag the boy away from Johnson, his gun still rock steady, pointed in the centre of Johnson's forehead.

'Please, please,' the mother pleaded repeatedly.

'Do what you've got to do. But let my family go,' Johnson said, looking defiantly back at him.

Danny stared back, his face emotionless, a cold unforgiving look in his eyes.

'Would you?' he said.

Downstairs in the kitchen, Lucus heard three shots from somewhere above him. He pushed himself painfully up the wall until he was upright, nearly falling back down when he had to snap the rifle up at the sound of someone moving towards him. He breathed a sigh of relief as Danny entered the kitchen.

'You got him? He's dead?' Lucus said through painful gasps.

'Trust me, you're never going to hear from Oliver Johnson again,' Danny answered, putting his arm around Lucus to help him out of the villa.

As they moved down the drive towards the Qashqai, Lucus looked over his shoulder to see the villa going up in flames.

Danny left a message for Hank as they drove towards Aviano Air Base.

Mission accomplished. Lucus has been wounded and needs medical attention. ETA Aviano Air Base in 35 minutes.

The reply came back in ten.

The 31st Medical Group has been alerted and will meet you at the gate.

'Hey Lucas, you still with me, mate?'

'Yeah, just resting my eyes,' Lucus replied, his face looking pale and the cleaning cloths secured to the wound with cling film were now soaked in blood.

'Good, not long now. Your boss has got a medical team waiting to take care of you, ok?'

When Lucus didn't answer, Danny looked across to see him pale and still with his eyes shut.

'Lucus, Lucus!' Danny shouted, reaching across to punch him in the bullet wound.

'Jesus, fuck!' Lucus screamed, sitting upright, pain written all over his face.

'Sorry, mate, you've lost a lot of blood. I just need you to stay awake until we get there,' said Danny, relieved that he was still alive.

'Well, I'm sure as hell awake now,' he grimaced.

Danny put his foot down as much as he dared. Being stopped with unlicensed guns in the boot and a man injured with a bullet wound would lead to a prison sentence, however he tried to explain it. After half an hour that felt like two, they arrived at Aviano US Air Base. Lieutenant Kyle Brooks met them at the gate with members of the 31st Medical Group.

'Hey Pearson, sorry I misjudged you. You're one hell of a soldier,' Lucus said, as they prepared to transfer him to the hospital on the base.

'Not me, mate, I'm just a civilian,' Danny said, smiling

while giving Lucus the finger, which made him laugh, then wince in pain.

'If you'd like to come with me, Mr Pearson, we'll take care of your vehicle and I'll find you some clothes before you get on your flight back to England,' said Lieutenant Brooks.

Danny looked down, noticing for the first time the blood-stains all over his clothes.

'Yeah, that might be a good idea,' he said, already thinking about Nikki's reaction at his disappearance.

CHAPTER 62

Danny opened the front door to his house, slowly poking his head inside first to see if Nikki was about. As he entered the hall, he held the latch and closed the door silently behind him. He headed towards the kitchen, freezing to the spot when a voice came from the living room to his left.

'Where the hell have you been?'

'Ah, hang on, love, I know you're probably angry with me just disappearing on you, but there wasn't any time to discuss it. Simon found the location of Tom and John's killer and I had a small window of opportunity to get him,' Danny said, hoping his explanation would soften the furious look Nikki had fixed on him.

'Get him? What does that actually mean? Definitely not arrest him, because last time I looked you're not a policeman and you sure as hell don't carry handcuffs. You mean kill him, don't you?'

Danny looked at her, wishing that he'd refused Simon's offer and let someone else deal with Johnson.

'Yes, I went there to kill him,' he replied softly. He loved Nikki and wasn't about to lie to her again.

Nikki's anger turned to emotional upset. She sat back down on the sofa and put her head in her hands and sobbed.

'You killed him for revenge. Murdered him. What kind of husband does that make you? What kind of father does that?' she said through the tears.

'He's not dead. I didn't kill him. I let him go,' Danny said, dropping to his knees to cradle Nikki.

Nikki lifted her head slowly and looked him in the eyes.

'You didn't kill him?'

'No, I didn't kill him.'

Nikki dried her eyes and put her arms around him, hugging him tight. At that point, something Nikki said earlier hit him like a ton of bricks.

'Wait, what? Did you say what kind of father?' he said, moving back to look at her face.

'Yes, that's why I've been feeling sick and emotional lately. I'm pregnant. We're going to have a baby,' she replied, a concerned look spreading across her face. She wiped the tears away and waited for Danny's reaction to the news.

There was a pause for a few seconds while he let her words sink in.

'That's bloody fantastic! I love you, Nichola Pearson. I'm going to be a dad,' he said, grinning, the atmosphere lifting in the room as he leaned in and gave her a passionate kiss.

'Really, you're happy about it?' Nikki said, relieved that he hadn't killed Johnson for revenge, and relieved that he was so happy about being a father again after his first son was killed in a car crash years ago.

Later that day, when everything had calmed down, Danny was in the kitchen, his thoughts returning to the room with his gun pointed at Johnson's head, and the little boy with the soft brown eyes being torn from his father by Johnson's wife while she begged him not to kill her husband.

'Do what you've got to do. But let my family go,' Johnson said, looking defiantly back at him.

Danny stared back, his face emotionless, with a cold look in his eyes.

'Would you?' he said coldly.

Danny's trigger finger applied pressure on the metal, but stopped short of pulling it back. Try as he might, Danny couldn't shut the image of Johnson's boy out of his head as he stared at him with big, brown, frightened eyes.

'You and your family are going to disappear. Just get in your car and vanish. Do you understand me?' Danny said, relaxing his grip on the gun before dropping it to his side.

Johnson's look changed from a condemned man to one with new hope as he nodded at Danny.

'If I hear that you've been operating again, I will come for you and I will kill you.'

'You won't, it's over,' Johnson said, getting painfully to his feet, his wife and son moving to his side and clinging on to him.

Danny pointed his gun away from them and squeezed off three rounds into the wall.

'I'll tell them you're dead. Now go, get out of here,' Danny said.

Johnson spoke to his family in Italian and ushered them out of the room, turning in the doorway to look back at Danny.

'Thank you.'

'I didn't do it for you. I did it for your family. Take care of them,' Danny replied solemnly.

'I will,' Johnson nodded before disappearing out of sight.

Danny waited a few minutes, then set fire to the first floor of the house before moving downstairs to help Lucus out to the car.

'You got him? He's dead?' Lucus said through painful gasps.

'Trust me, you're never going to hear from Oliver Johnson again.'

'Penny for them,' Nikki said, entering the kitchen to see Danny staring out the window, his mind a million miles away.

'What? Oh, nothing. I was just thinking we'd better tell everyone our good news.'

'Ah, well, Tina already knows, which probably means your brother Rob knows.'

'Ok, well, we'd better tell Scott then.'

The doorbell rang and Nikki scooted off to answer it.

'Er, well, when you disappeared, I was upset and I kind of told Scott,' she shouted back from the hall.

'Oh great, is there anyone who didn't know about this before me?' Danny grumbled, following Nikki into the hall to see who was at the door.

'Aunty Nikki's having a baby,' yelled his niece Sophie, running towards him ahead of his brother Rob, Tina and baby George.

'No, I guess not,' Danny muttered, picking up Sophie and accepting the congratulations from Rob and Tina as they came in carrying a bottle of bubbly and beers.

'Watch out, here comes Uncle Scotty,' shouted Scott, following the others inside. 'God, I hope it has your looks, sis. We wouldn't want it looking like the caveman over there.'

'Yeah, alright, very funny, Scott,' Danny chuckled.

'Seriously, old man, congratulations. I'm thrilled for you.'

'Thanks, Scotty boy, now get yourself a drink before you have me in tears,' Danny chuckled, grabbing a beer off Rob as he went by.

CHAPTER 63

After a month of lying low in Geneva waiting for his face to heal and his new identity papers, Alfred Birchwood was relaxing in a five-star hotel in the Philippines. He intended to stay another week or two before travelling to Cape Town to buy a property and rebuild his life under his new South African identity. He finished breakfast, telling the restaurant ma"tre d to charge it to his room before heading through the foyer on his way to the beach.

'Mr Bekka, may I have a quick word, please?' came the voice of the manager from behind the reception desk, stopping him in his tracks.

'Yes,' Birchwood said abruptly, still trying to get used to being called by his new name Bekka.

'Sorry, sir, there seems to be a problem with the card details you gave us. The payment has been declined,' the manager spoke politely but with a certain amount of insistence in his voice.

'What? Impossible! Run it again.'

'We did, sir, several times,' the manager replied, pulling the bill and several declined payment receipts from behind the desk.

'There's got to be some sort of error. I will talk to my bank and get it sorted out,' said Birchwood, dismissing the manager as he turned to leave.

'I'm sorry, sir, I must insist the bill is settled now.'

Birchwood turned and glared at the manager. He was about to protest further when the sight of hotel security men appearing near the reception desk stopped him from making a scene.

'Fine, here, charge it to this card,' he said, pulling one of the many bank cards from his wallet.

'Thank you, sir,' the manager replied politely, taking the card and putting the details through the payment screen on his computer.

Birchwood stood impatiently drumming the reception desk with his fingers, his mind thinking about the blasting he was going to give the bank for causing him this incon-venience.

'Sorry, sir, that has been declined as well.'

'What? That's impossible. What the hell's going on? It must be your system that's faulty.'

'I assure you, Mr Bekka, our system is working fine.'

Not so sure of himself anymore, Birchwood pulled another card from his wallet and slapped it down on the reception desk. When the manager ran it through the system and shook his head, Birchwood stepped back from the desk gobsmacked.

'This is obviously some kind of mistake. I'm going to my room to sort this out right now,' Birchwood blurted out as confidently as he could, before heading away from the desk to dash up the stairs.

'Mr Bekka, would you mind coming back here?'

When Birchwood didn't respond and increased his pace up the stairs, the manager gave a nod to his security team who headed up the stairs after him. As soon as Birchwood was out of sight of the reception, he broke into a run, taking the stairs two at a time before turning down the corridor and sprinting to his hotel suite. He entered the room, shutting the door and twisting the deadbolt in place behind him. Breathing heavily, he ran to the desk and opened his laptop, frantically logging into his online bank accounts.

'No, no, no,' he cried in desperation, hardly hearing the bangs on the door as each account came back 'Account balance zero' time and time again.

'Mr Bekka, please open the door or we will have to enter forcibly.'

Birchwood wasn't listening. He looked around the suite in a state of shock, a frown forming on his face as his eyes fell on a brown leather satchel that didn't belong to him sitting on a chair in the room's corner. As the hotel security guards started to break the door down, Birchwood went over to the satchel and opened it. He reached in and pulled out a gun in one hand, looking at it like he was in a bad dream. Birchwood could see something else inside the satchel and reached in to pull a bag of white power out with the other hand. He was still standing there in disbelief when the door lock gave way and hotel security burst in. Birchwood turned to face them, the gun and bag of white powder still in his hands. The guards reacted quickly by diving on top of him, pinning him to the ground. With his protests of innocence falling on deaf ears, Birchwood remained restrained on the carpet until the police arrived and took him to the station. After being processed, they placed him in a holding cell where he sat in the corner, trying to avoid the intimidating stares of ten hard looking men crammed in with him. After four hours of sitting in the stifling heat with the smell of stale sweat and piss, Birchwood sat drenched in sweat and on the verge of a breakdown.

'Bekka, Frances Bekka, come to the front.'

It took a few seconds for Birchwood to realise they were calling him. The tiniest thread of hope that there had been a mistake and they were going to release him sent him rushing to the front.

'Yes, yes, that's me, Frances Bekka.'

The police officer's uninterested look gave nothing away. He unlocked the barred door to the cell and opened it.

'Come with me,' he said, the other prisoners piping up as he slammed the door shut and locked it behind him. He yelled something in his native tongue which seemed to quiet them down, then led Birchwood through the police station to a windowless interview room, pushing him roughly into a chair before leaving him alone in the bare, grey room, lit only by a flickering bulkhead screwed to the centre of the ceiling.

After leaving him there for what felt like ages, the clang of the heavy metallic lock being turned made him jump. The door swung open and an immaculately dressed man in a blue suit walked confidently into the room. Birchwood thought it might be a lawyer for him until his eyes adjusted and the man's facial features became clear.

'You!' he said through gritted teeth.

'Good afternoon, er, Mr Bekka, isn't it?' Simon said, pausing to look at Birchwood's new identity for dramatic effect before continuing. 'My, my, my, trying to run out on your hotel bill, carrying an unlicensed weapon and drug smuggling. That's quite the full set of charges. The Philippine justice system takes this kind of thing very seriously. You'll be lucky if you ever see the outside world again.'

'You set me up, you bastard. What did you do with my money?' Birchwood spat back.

'That's an interesting turn of phrase, your money. I think you'll find it belongs to the British government, which is exactly where it is now,' Simon continued, his voice calm, as always. A small smile forming as he spoke.

'But how? I had everything covered, there's no way you could have got to it.'

'Me, no. But to reduce his sentence, Tobias Valentine —

you remember him, the young man you had groomed to do your dirty work — well, Mr Valentine has been only too happy to use his, quite frankly, brilliant talents to piece together the tiniest pieces of data to trace our money and your location. Then we got him to hack your accounts. Quite ironic if you think about it.'

'You can't do this. You framed me, planted the gun and drugs in my room. I want a lawyer. I'll tell everyone what you've done to me. I'm a British citizen, for Christ's sake.' Birchwood shouted across the interview room table at Simon.

Simon stood up slowly, without reacting to Birchwood's outburst. He paused for a moment to open the file in his hand before answering.

'I'm sorry, Mr Bekka, it says here you're a South African national. Maybe you should give the South African embassy a call,' said Simon, shutting the file and walking over to the door. He gave it a knock and waited for the police officer to open it. Pausing in the doorway, Simon turned to look at Birchwood before leaving.

'Goodbye, Alfred,' he said, stepping out into the corridor.

The police officer slammed the interview room door shut before escorting Simon towards the exit, Birchwood's muffled hysterical cry echoing down the corridor behind him. 'You can't do this. I'm innocent. You can't leave me here.'

CHOOSE YOUR NEXT NOVEL

Vodka Over London Ice

The London mob clash with the Russian Mafia. The death and violence escalate, putting Danny's family in danger. Danny Pearson has to end the war, before more family die…

Execution of Faith

Terrorists and mercenary killers plot to change the balance of world power. Can Danny Pearson stop them or will this be his downfall…

Who Holds The Power

As a Secret organisation kills, corrupts and influences its way to global domination. Danny Pearson must stop them and their deadly Chinese assassin in his most dangerous adventure to date…

Alive Until I Die

When government cutbacks threaten project Dragonfly. General Rufus McManus takes direct action to secure its future. Deep undercover with his life on the line, can Danny survive long enough to bring him to justice…

Sport of Kings

When Danny's old SAS buddy goes missing, Danny's unit reunite to find him. When they follow Smudges trail they find themselves on the wrong side of an international drug smuggling operation and the sport of kings, an exclusive hunt of a deadly nature…

Blood Runs Deep

Five Years Ago (Vodka Over London Ice) The London mob clashed with the Russian Mafia. Death and violence escalated, putting Danny's family in danger. Danny Pearson ended the war, or so he thought…

Command To Kill

When Australian billionaire Theodore Blazer takes advantage of todays plugged in world with sinister intentions, Danny travels to the far side of the globe to stop the world falling apart.

No Upper Limit

Journalist David Wallace is killed when he tries to find out the identity of an arms dealer known as the Wolf, Danny Pearson's SAS unit is also trying to stop the Wolf selling arms to the Taliban. When they get close the Wolf disappears forever, or so they thought…

Leave Nothing To Chance

When Danny's best friend Scott goes missing from his hotel room in Brazil, Danny pulls out all the stops to find him. The search takes him into the heart of Colombia and the clutches of a drugs baron known as El Diablo.

Won't Stay Dead

Snipe's back, awoken from his coma and with no recollection of the past few years. When the facility recondition him and put him to work, everything is fine until his memory and insanity return.

Till Death Do Us Part

Danny, his best friend Scott and his old SAS buddies travel to Benidorm for his stag do, what could possibly go wrong.

Enemy At The Door

Disillusioned with the government, the state of the planet, and their future prospects, a group of the countries elite university students take matters into their own hands. With money, power and connections they kick their campaign of terror off by blowing up The Red Lion Pub on Parliament Street.

Whatever It Takes

When Danny's old SAS friend Fergus has his daughter Kirsty taken by a Slovenian people trafficking gang, Danny, Chaz and Scott come to his aid.

ABOUT THE AUTHOR

Stephen Taylor spent over twenty years wiring up homes and businesses with audio visual kit before the big 50 started looming and he finally sat down to write the book he'd always had rattling around in his head. That book was *Execution of Faith* — a supercharged, no-nonsense thriller that hit the ground running and never looked back. Readers loved it so much he wrote a prequel, *Vodka Over London Ice*, which became the first in what is now the internationally bestselling Danny Pearson series.

Raised on a diet of Lee Child's Jack Reacher, Vince Flynn's Mitch Rapp, and Tom Wood's Victor — with a healthy side serving of Die Hard, Daniel Craig's Bond, and anything Guy Ritchie ever pointed a camera at — Stephen writes the kind of thrillers he wants to read: hard, fast, no filler, and with enough humour to keep you grinning between the gunfights.

The Danny Pearson series has found fans across the world who love action that doesn't let up and a hero who's as handy with a one-liner as he is with his fists. If you like your thrillers with the throttle wide open, you're in the right place.